Fitzmaurice Okeden

Philip Vaughan's Marriage

Vol. 1

Fitzmaurice Okeden

Philip Vaughan's Marriage
Vol. 1

ISBN/EAN: 9783337346522

Printed in Europe, USA, Canada, Australia, Japan

Cover: Foto ©Andreas Hilbeck / pixelio.de

More available books at **www.hansebooks.com**

PHILIP VAUGHAN'S MARRIAGE.

A NOVEL.

IN TWO VOLUMES.

BY

Mrs. FITZMAURICE OKEDEN,

Author of "Felicia's Dowry."

"Bid your friends."
As You Like It, Act V.

VOL. I.

London:
T. CAUTLEY NEWBY, PUBLISHER,
30, WELBECK STREET, CAVENDISH SQUARE.
1869.

TO MY COUSIN

HELENA

(MRS. ALFRED WATNEY),

MY SECOND NOVEL IS DEDICATED WITH AFFECTION.

BOOK I.

——

THE BOARDING-HOUSE.

PHILIP VAUGHAN'S MARRIAGE.

CHAPTER I.

AN ARRIVAL.

On an evening late in the August of 183—, when the scarlet berries of the mountain ash were looking gay at the roadside, a horseman turned his back upon the little Welsh town of B——th, glanced in the direction of the sinking sun, took a short, but more general survey of the sky, and commenced a steady trot against the hill.

Notwithstanding that he could not easily

have been better mounted, the light was failing by the time he drew rein near a few hovels on the edge of a common of consider-able extent. The immediate scene found no favour in his eyes, and a few words may des-cribe it. On the one hand he had a small farm-house—such a farm-house as he might have ridden over many fair English counties to find ; on the other, less than half a dozen poorer huts, including the blacksmith's forge. The fire from this last reddened a group of three-parts naked children squatted round the building, and watching the smith's work on the shoe of a rough galloway, whose owner— a young fellow in a velveteen shooting-jacket —leaned against the wall of the forge, and exchanged a word now and then with a girl hard by. A pig, apparently unsatisfied with his supper, and three or four fowls, whose meagre and ill-clad bodies rather indicated self-help and habitual irregularity of hours than anything else, were entities not to be overlooked in this little evening reunion approached by the horseman, and regarded from the doorway of one of the hovels by a middle-aged and well-featured woman, with an infant in her arms. It was a scene unlovely, as I have already said, in the eyes that now saw it for the first time ; nor rendered less so by the heavy clouds that, succeeding the sunset, had massed themselves grandly above the horizon, and threatened to overspread the whole sky.

The clink of the smith's hammer ceased, and the children became silent as the stranger drew near. The girl, too, turned her head to look at him, when he rode up, and asked his distance from Ll——d.

" From Old Ll——d ?" counter-asked the man.

" 'Tis the Wells, Owen," said the girl.

" Two mile, sure, sir !" This time the eldest woman spoke, for a dog was barking furiously, and the smith's English was at fault. The stranger looked around him at the weather, and with a gesture—a very slight one—of acknowledgment of the information he had received, rode on.

A sharp trot of a few minutes brought him in sight of what seemed a shabby clump of trees, at the further side of the common; and, presently, he could catch glimpses of a house amidst these trees. He quickened his pace, and in the moment after, discovered that he was overtaking some object moving more slowly than himself in the same direction. He had soon ridden by a group of three ladies and a gentleman, and left behind, a little farther on, another gentleman and lady who stood perfectly still to regard him. A few heavy drops of rain fell as he reached and passed through a gateway, forming the entrance to a sort of rude avenue that led, he supposed, direct to the house. And now he trotted along this path, emerged from the shadow of the trees, and found himself in front of the principal boarding house of Ll——d Wells.

This, at the time of which I write, gave little indication in its outward appearance of

the comforts of an ordinary hotel. It was a
small, square building, having on its right
the stables and stable-yard, with bed-rooms
for servants above; and in 'front a gravelled
sweep surrounding a grass plot, in the centre of
which was a large tree. The ground rose a
little to the spring—whose exact distance
from the house I do not now remember, but
it was trifling—and at this spot there was a
small roofed shelter for the water-drinkers,
forming the boundary at one end of a straight
walk, of which an arbour was the terminus
at the other. Beyond the arbour was a gate,
and a path across the common.

Yet, notwithstanding its unpretending
aspect, this place was, every year, the scene
of more merriment, more flirtation, more
giddy friendships, more light loves—aye, and
sometimes more serious matches, too—than
many possessing twenty-times its attractions.
The absence of ordinary luxuries within doors,
inclined people to be a good deal out. Walks
and rides brought them acquainted; and those

who walked and rode together in the morning, easily found themselves singing, dancing, and playing cards together at night. So that the young passed pleasant days at Ll——d Wells ; and the old were able to desire a good deal of entertainment from what was going on around them ; became imbued with the general willingness to make the best of everything, and really passed—some of them even very cross old persons—pleasant days there too.

But this was only in the summer months. The appearance of bad weather quickly dispersed the smiles both of old and young, and very soon after, the people themselves. I speak of prevailing bad weather. As to a wet morning or afternoon, now and then, or even very occasionally a whole rainy day— these have been known to advance a flirtation ; nay, to bring one already arrived at a certain growth, to the perfected maturity of a proposal which in the more occupied fine season might never have been made. Pre-

vailing bad weather, then, was not pleasant
at Ll——d Wells; and during the August of
this year of which I write, bad weather had
prevailed. The summer party (a gay one of
young men and girls, with just sufficient
chaperonage, male and female, to interpose
the little difficulties and restrictions that make
matters more eagerly enjoyed) had broken
up earlier than usual; and when the stranger
rode into the stable-yard, but three persons
assembled at the window of the sitting-room
to pronounce upon the new comer. These
were a spectacled elderly gentleman, and two
ladies, not less advanced in years than himself. There was a suspicion, however, of a
gayer-looking cap in a remoter part of the
room, and the stranger—if he were a stranger
inclining to society—probably reminded himself of the groups he had passed on the common.

It may be as well here briefly to introduce
to the reader the persons composing the now

very limited party remaining at this late season at the Ll——d Wells.

They might, indeed, be better divided into *two* parties ; the three or four individuals not attached to either being mere walking ladies and gentlemen on a stage where more important characters have parts to play.

Of these two parties, then. In point of strength they were very nicely balanced; but in respect of numbers there was sufficient inequality ; for while the one party consisted only of a lady and her daughter, the other included no fewer than eight persons.

But then, Lady Jones was more than seven persons in herself. She was supposed by the company at the Ll——d Wells to have mixed in the first circles in London and elsewhere; and, in fact, it was known that she had been presented at Court. She had, besides, it was considered, quite the air of a woman of fashion, and possessed several anecdotes of fine people, none of them, perhaps, particularly witty, but all tending to show that those fine people had the greatest possible consideration for Lady Jones.

I confess I had, at some rare times, the hardihood to think it a little strange that a lady so valued in the first circles in London and other places equally distant and desirable, should find pleasure in returning to spend summer after summer on the same comparatively obscure spot. At first sight, the waters seemed to offer a rational solution of the problem; but then—Lady Jones did not drink them. Of air, too, she inhaled very little; still, when she did sally forth, she invariably declared this last did her a monstrous deal of good, and one certainly did not feel disposed to doubt it. The objection I have named, however, did not I believe occur to the habitual frequenters of the Wells themselves. And then—and to conclude the matter—Lady Jones never did seem pleased.

Of Miss Jones I need only say, that if her mother were rather more than seven persons, she was rather less than one.

But at the head of the opposite party—I call it the opposite party because, though the two did in a manner coalesce for mutual respectability and convenience, there was much cordial dislike entertained by each towards the other—at the head of the opposite party was a lady in all respects extremely dissimilar to Lady Jones. This was a full-blown personage, past her youth, but who had still large claims to a certain admiration. She had superb eyes and eyebrows, fine teeth, and wore very becoming caps. She had, too, a husband and a son ; and there was, besides these, a brother of her husband who paid her very proper attention.

Mrs. Fleming was, on the whole, a different looking person from the married and single ladies who were accustomed to visit the Wells ; and though it would be too much to say that these held themselves aloof from her, they really did not seem quite at their ease in her company. She, on her part, had the air of desiring to appear perfectly happy with them ;

notwithstanding which, her manner was most natural when gentlemen happened to preponderate in her circle. She had with her a young lady who wore long ringlets, and who was near her on all occasions.

Under the head of this party I have to notice three other persons, because, though they did not arrive with it (indeed they had preceded its arrival by quite three weeks), the two groups amalgamated and became only one immediately, and had evidently been extremely good friends before the date of their meeting at the boarding-house of Ll——d Wells.

These three persons were, a sullen-looking but handsome man, his wife, and a pale young lady, the cousin of the latter. I shall defer giving any further description of these three persons till the next chapter; only, in concluding this one it may be as well to mention that in the course of the week by which the arrival of Mrs. Fleming and her friends had been beforehand with that of the horseman whose existence is not, we hope, forgotten by the reader, the handsome man had on several occasions presented his arm to the young person with the ringlets, and the brother of Mrs. Fleming's husband had become particularly the ally of Mrs. Robert Spender.

CHAPTER II.

THE NEW MAN.

ABOUT a quarter of an hour after the person
newly arrived had been installed, together
with a portmanteau left that morning by the
Brecon coach, in an apartment commonly de-
signated "the Post-chaise," the adjoining room
was entered by the pale young lady already mentioned, who proceeded to divest herself of her
bonnet and rearrange her hair.   She appeared
a little fluttered, which—considering her run
home in the rain—was not, perhaps, very

strange; but, beyond this, she paused more than once in twisting a bit of purple heath into a sort of coronet for her head, and glanced apprehensively round the room.

Presently there came a footstep to the door, and a knock. The footstep was a light one, and the knock in itself by no means alarming; nevertheless, the pale lady turned paler still, and paused for some few seconds before she bid the applicant " come in."

There entered, with a candle in her hand —for it was by this time dark—a person about the age of the first occupant of the apartment. She was not very pretty, but had a look of prettiness ; and while her attire was extremely simple, the effect was that she was a good deal dressed. This was, possibly, because she was a good deal undressed. I am writing, I must beg you to remember, of the year 183—, when ladies rarely appeared as uncovered as they may be seen at present, but were so to a certain extent on more ordinary occasions. She was, then, for the fashion of that day a good deal undressed;

and though, as I have said, she was not really pretty, she had an air of attractiveness, which is sometimes, especially in a young married woman, almost the same thing.

"I came in, my dear, to say"—animatedly commenced this person, who was Mrs. Robert Spender—"but how odd you look! Is anything the matter?"

"No,—a little! I overran myself, I believe. In a minute I will be ready to go down with you.   Good God!" she exclaimed, agitatedly, "there can be no one in the room?"

"Impossible!—I protest you startled me. If you hear anything it must be in the next room.   There!—it is the new man: they have put him in the 'Post-chaise.'   Heavens, Julia! *is* anything the matter?"

"Nothing!" Julia replied.   "But I have not felt like this for years."

"How disgustingly strange!—and you know there can be no one in the room, it is so small—not a cupboard even, you see," and she lifted up the little dimity vallance of the bed; "there is only your trunk. Tears in your eyes! My dear creature, you are not well. Stay here quietly, and let me send you up some tea: it was stupid to take so long a walk. As I live, there is the bell already, and Miss Eliza Smith is, I suppose, making herself conspicuous with my husband for the delectation of the company. I hope I may be forgiven, Ju, if I wrong that girl, but —have you a pin I can put in this bow? I believe she is quite as good friends with Robert as she need be."

"My dear Diana!" said the pale lady.

"Well—I may be mistaken. She had better look to herself, however. It is very little her fault that I am Mrs. Robert at this moment, so I only advise her to be careful."

"I never even thought," said Julia, "that your husband admired her."

"Certainly not,—and he abominates red hair! Yet you must have been rather in the clouds not to have seen the goings-on of the last few days. He would have no motive but the very idlest amusement! Well! I will send Phœbe with some tea, and will find ten minutes afterwards to run up and see how you are. Perhaps I shall be able to tell you something about the new man. For goodness' sake, light another candle!" And away ran Mrs. Robert Spender.

Society at the Wells drank tea in the same room in which it breakfasted and dined. It sat at the same long table; was summoned by the same very discordant bell; and was quite as hungry as at either of the two earlier reunions of the day. It was much the custom for a person newly arrived to present himself to the said society at the time of one of these reunions, under cover, as it were, of the little bustle created by the entrance of the visitors from all quarters upon the scene of action. The non-appearance, therefore, of the stranger on the present occasion was productive of a general feeling of disappointment.

A close observer could not have failed to note the little air of a toilette rather more *soignée* than usual that prevailed amongst the ladies ; and Mrs. Robert Spender not only noted but remarked upon the emancipation of an unaccustomed ringlet from the comb that confined Miss Eliza Smith's back hair. The young single lady coloured uneasily, for the remark elicited an involuntary side-look at the ringlet in question from Mr. Robert Spender ; a look which might have been translated to mean that as the ringlet was so nearly red, it might very well have been left where it was before. I am writing, you must again be reminded, of a period when auburn, whether in hair or whiskers, was less the fashion than it is now : when it was looked upon rather as a deformity than otherwise ; when Byron was still quoted, and " Philip " had not appeared. And *red*, be it said in justice, Miss Eliza Smith's hair was not. Mrs. Robert Spender had calumniated it. Ladies who had dark hair themselves were liable to such exaggerations : the more innocent in this instance as the young person was especially distinguished by the peculiar shade, or rather *no* shade, of eyebrow and eye-lash, and a certain floridness of skin, without distinct colour, which generally accompany tresses after the Roman taste; so that Mrs. Robert Spender's observation was really not inexcusable.

On this evening, notwithstanding that each person was perfectly polite to the others, there did not seem to prevail the entire harmony that a philanthropist might have desired. Mrs. Fleming and her party had stayed out late, and the boarding-house people, in compliment to so much the larger number of the guests, had taken upon themselves to delay the summons to tea till their return: and that this delay had given umbrage to Lady Jones was perceivable in a certain augmented elegance of her ladyship's demeanour, and in the particular and pointed inquiries she addressed to Mrs. Fleming on the subject of her walk,—while the latter lady, on her part, was disconcerted at being so singled out.

Tea, however, progressed, and came to a conclusion; and it was subsequently discovered that the person newly arrived had in the meanwhile eaten his dinner in the commercial—otherwise, the bagman's room, and had returned to his apartment, and that candles had been conveyed thither by his desire.

" Alas! young ladies!" said Mrs. Robert Spender.

About half-past nine o'clock in the evening, Lady Jones, Mrs. Fleming, Master Fleming, the spectacled gentleman (a Mr. Morgan) already mentioned, and two elderly Misses Davies (who, on the tea question, had considered Lady Jones ill-used), were engaged in a round game. Miss Eliza Smith and Mr. Robert Spender were lookers-on, or to be supposed such. Mrs. Robert sat near a little table at which Miss Jones was working; and a book had been ostensibly chosen by the young married lady for the amusement of her evening. She had, however, laid it down to talk to Major and Captain Fleming, both of whom had placed themselves near her. I hope I have given you an idea of the interior of the boarding-house sitting-room at half-past nine o'clock in the evening, for about that hour the door opened, and the stranger walked in.

Every eye turned upon him, and at the same time every voice ceased; but, if the position were an embarrassing one, never had man less the air of feeling himself embarrassed. His regards went quietly round the room, and fell for a moment on Miss Jones. That young lady, however, glanced in the direction of her mother, and averted her head. The next person on whom they rested—I am speaking of the stranger's regards—was Mrs. Robert Spender, and probably they met with more encouragement, for he approached her.

He approached her under a terrific fire from the card-table; and her cavaliers turning their attention at the moment to Miss Jones, and a little entanglement of the work table and empty chairs giving the young married lady occasion to make some trifling movement of civility in favour of the " new man," it was in a very short time that Lady Jones beheld (be it said with more indignation than astonishment) Mrs. Robert and that "new man" talking and laughing together as if—to use her ladyship's expression —as if they had been acquainted since the flood.

Lady Jones would have been more indignant if, after the first quarter of an hour, she could have overheard the conversation.

" You forget," said Diana, " that I have already been guilty of an immense impropriety. Only ask Lady Jones! I do not even know what to call you."

" I fear," responded the gentleman, whom fifteen minutes' conversation had probably made tolerably well acquainted with the style of Mrs. Robert Spender, "I fear," he responded, with a slight downward glance in the direction of the white hand nearest to him, "you may not consider yourself at liberty to call me yours."

"Impossible!" said the lady. "See!" and she raised the finger encircled by her wedding ring, which last she coquettishly kissed.

"That kiss, at any rate," said the gentleman, "settles the matter. Then, call me Featherstone."

"Mr.?—good Heavens! Lord Featherstone?"

Lord Featherstone bowed; and it was a bow that it took Mrs. Robert Spender a quarter of a minute to recover from,—it and the surprise.

At the end of that time, "Mercy on us!" she exclaimed. "Are you at all prepared for the sensation you will make? That wretched old woman will be out of herself."

"Which wretched old woman?"

"Can you inquire? Already her disgust at my effrontery is beginning to give place to terror, lest you should be anything better than a bagman. Do you not see? she fears her prudence may have been too great for the occasion, and glances uneasily in the direction of her daughter. Absolutely, I compassionate her state of mind just now."

Lord Featherstone laughed rather heartily, and in fact, Lady Jones was to be pitied. Some covert glances in the direction of the person with whom Mrs. Robert Spender was talking, had made her aware that he was a fashionable looking man; and a certain air of repressed satire and scarcely repressed amusement with which his eye—an experienced looking eye—rested from time to time on the party of which she herself made one, caused her to move uneasily on her chair.

" And this is the circle?" asked Lord Featherstone.

" With one exception; a cousin of my own who is not down stairs to-night."

" An invalid ?"

"Oh! no. Only she was nervous this evening, and remained in her own room. By the way, she is a next neighbour of yours."

" And you will not let me be of your riding party to this charming place with the
unpronounceable name to-morrow?"

" Nay, I have not said so.   Major Fleming
—Captain Fleming," and she turned to those
gentlemen, " will you help me to ask Lord
Featherstone to join our riding party to
Abbey Cwm Hîr ?"

This appeal served to recall both the persons to whom it was addressed, and include
them in the conversation; and presently—the
round game being at an end—Lady Jones had
the annoyance of beholding Mrs. Fleming,
her son, Mr. Spender, and even the young
lady with the ringlets, severally join the circle
of Mrs. Robert, in which the words " Lord
Featherstone" were more than once audible
to her ladyship's ear.

Beholding this, and dissatisfied with her
own unwonted position in the back ground,
she approached her daughter, drew that young
person's arm within her own, and went forward to make her evening compliments to the

group.   These offered, she courtesied benignly to the stranger, who acknowledged the salutation by a profound bow.   Then, conceiving she had made the *amende*, and that it had been accepted, her ladyship walked out at the door—held open for her by young Fleming — with dignity and satisfactio n blended.

When the company had retired, and Lord Featherstone found himself once more in his room, he did not betake himself immediately to bed, but sate down and wrote as follows :—

"Pump House, Ll——d Wells,
" August 30th, 183—.

" Well, Fred! I have made my journey, and am here.

" As a matter of course, I have not seen her.   You will conceive that I am not desirous of gratifying the select company at the boarding-house with a scene of any sort whatsoever.   Nevertheless, I have been below.

" I have seen and conversed with the cousin, and am absolutely unrecognised by her. You see my estimate of the change effected by eleven years, a tropical climate, and a scarred lip (not to mention the light *peruke* which I have duly adopted, though I believe the precaution unnecessary), was a better one than yours. Still, it is not in public that I must meet Julia for the first time. Her health is delicate, it seems. She has been sufficiently ill-used; however, there is ' a good time coming.'

" It formed no part of my original intention to put myself into the hands of the Philistines this night at least. I had even got lights up here, and my paper before me to write to you, when lo !—a voice. For eleven years I had not heard it, yet how familiar it sounded! I listened, and discovered that she occupied the apartment adjoining mine, and that she was in conversation with her cousin. They spoke low, but I found from a few words uttered by the latter as she left the room, that Julia did not mean to go down stairs that night.

"My first impulse was then, in the same moment, to present myself to her; but the briefest reflection convinced me that it would be an act of madness. The surprise, the hour, her delicacy of health—at once I abandoned the idea.

" From the few sentences I exchanged with Diana—I beg her pardon, with Mrs Robert Spender—I gather that she is precisely the person I knew formerly. Her character is not a difficult one to understand. She has some malice, some warmth of heart, some wit, and a good deal of effrontery. In person she is very decidedly improved. I imagine that she is married rather happily than otherwise, but finds flirtation quite as necessary to her existence as she did eleven years ago, and has always *beaucoup de penchant* for being admired.

"You are impatient, you say, for my interview with Julia. Well, for the present adieu! To-morrow will be a new day.

"Yours,

"FEATHERSTONE."

CHAPTER III.

"WE BOWED."

WHEN Lord Featherstone drew aside the curtain of his window on the morning after his arrival at Ll——d Wells, he found that the company had already assembled on the principal walk, where it was promenading in groups of two or three persons together, and that this accounted for the profound silence that reigned throughout the house at eight o'clock.

He had no difficulty in discovering the bright

eyes of Mrs. Robert Spender under the simplest, but at the same time the most effective, hat upon the walk, and did not feel surprised to see that this hat was, as it were, the banner under which the majority of the gentlemen marched.

Lord Featherstone made his toilet in no undue hurry; still, when he descended the stairs it wanted some minutes of nine. As his foot quitted the last step a lady was seen to approach the house from the Well, and perceiving this he turned into the drawing-room, which was on his left hand. Now the sun was shining very gaily into this apartment, and, as he stood near the window, a strong light was thrown upon his face and person. He had not been standing there more than two or three minutes when the door was opened by the lady he had observed coming towards the house, and who, seeing no one but the earl, bowed slightly to him and retired.

For a little while after this his lordship

remained looking from the window. Then the breakfast bell began to ring, and there was a rush of the company into the house.

You will already be prepared to hear that Mrs. Robert Spender was not the last person whom Lord Featherstone addressed, and that she did not fail to remind him of the riding engagement he had made the night before. It was a pity that the etiquette of the breakfast table separated them when they took their places. It did so, however, and Mrs. Robert had the greater leisure to remark a degree of pre-occupation in my lord's manner from which it had on the previous evening been absolutely free. Once she noticed his eye rest upon the pale young lady with a certain expression—I should perhaps rather say an uncertain one, for it puzzled her; and having seen this, she thought that while he conversed with Mrs. Fleming he had still the air of observing her cousin.

Ten minutes after the breakfast-room was empty, horses for the riding party appeared at the door; and ten minutes after the horses appeared at the door, the ladies were ready to mount them. Lord Featherstone counted them—the horses—as he stood on the step, his riding-whip in his hand. There were seven, including his own, and three of them had side saddles.

Just then Mr. Robert Spender came round at a quick pace from the stables. He went straight up to a handsome chestnut mare, quite evidently his, said a few words to the groom at her head, gave a momentary but keen eye to the general arrangements, and finally led her himself to the door.

That the creature was spirited all might perceive, that she was vicious some might suspect. Mrs. Robert had permitted herself to be witty on the subject of Miss Eliza Smith's horsewomanship, and it was perhaps this that had piqued her husband into a rather obstinate offer to the young unmarried lady of the beautiful animal in question.

"The mare," Mr. Spender said, "had no

vice," but was, on the contrary, rather more gentle than a lamb. Mrs. Robert had ridden her with perfect safety; why should not Miss Eliza Smith? Why, indeed? Unless it might happen that Mrs. Robert knew how to ride, and that Miss Eliza Smith did not.

By this time the greater part of the company had assembled at the door and windows, and it became evident even to very slightly experienced eyes that the person who was to mount Ruperta would gain nothing by delay. Mr. Spender, moreover, had taken the mouth of the mare under his own control, and was at no particular pains to conceal his impatience; Mr. Spender's wife expressed herself politely and perfectly satisfied to mount "after Miss Smith;" and Miss Smith was constrained to advance.

Ruperta was tall, and the young lady looked up to the saddle uneasily; Captain Fleming, always voluble in stable matters, and at the moment a little in the way, stood aside, and Mr. Spender's groom came forward.   Miss

Eliza Smith cast on him an imploring look; she grasped the pommel and the man lifted her foot. One foot, however, was all his province, so the other remained behind.

Mr. Robert Spender bit his lip, Mrs. Robert's eyes looked particularly bright, and the groom said—

" Keep your knee stiff, Miss—now !"

But the young lady's second attempt was as little to the purpose as the first, and the master of the astonished Ruperta, relinquishing her rein to a second groom, turned short round and walked away. Captain Fleming, on the contrary, ready for " all that may become a man," and being the shortest one present, said he could lift Miss Eliza Smith up, and essayed to do it, so ineffectually, however, that it was a mercy they were not both under the animal together.

In this emergency my Lord Featherstone suddenly made a step forward. Miss Eliza Smith was looking frightened, red, and almost in tears, and accepted his offer with a sort of despair of reaching the top of her horse at all. Yet he looked a person to rely upon, and, in fact, he had no sooner touched her foot than she found herself in the saddle; an end of her difficulties so unexpected that, uotwithstanding her ill-concealed uneasiness at sundry tossings, and shakings, and stampings on the part of the animal with respect to whom she occupied what she thought no very enviable position, she thanked the earl by a look so truly grateful that he discovered her features to be worthy of more attention than he had hitherto bestowed on them. When the little party moved off she found him at her side. Indeed, he remained there during the greatest part of the morning, and Mrs. Robert Spender, who had counted on him for her cavalier, saw her handsome husband detached from the young person in the last manner she desired.

The fair Diana possessed, however, too much self-command to betray the very least of her woman's pique on the occasion. Well mounted, perfectly at her ease in the saddle, conscious of the attractiveness of her small figure in an admirably fitting habit and faultless hat, she was the gaiety of the little party; and when, towards the conclusion of the ride, she found Lord Featherstone for the first time her companion, and that they were a little in advance of the rest, there was not a shade on her brow or a flat note in her voice that could lead him to suppose the morning had been in any way less satisfactory to her than it had seemed to be. Whether, without the help of these indices to the volume of a lady's mind, his lordship was able to peruse that of Mrs. Robert Spender, is another matter.

It was not very difficult for Mrs. Robert to render those last three miles more agreeable to the Earl than the previous ones had been. Miss Eliza Smith was far from clever, and, though her riding had not justified Mrs. Robert's contemptuous opinion of it, she was not at home on her horse. The organ that indicates satire was tolerably developed on the young married lady's pericranium, and possibly the suppressed pique of the morning had added some brilliancy to the sparks her wit struck from the interior of the Ll——d Wells boarding-house. To judge from Lord Featherstone's remark when they were almost within sight of their dinner, she had been quite as lively as good natured.

" There is one person you have spared," he said, " your cousin."

" That, " she replied," is another matter; she is a very different person, as you have observed, and I cannot paint her for you with the same brush I have used for the others. If any of the colours were to remain in it they would spoil the likeness."

" ' As I have observed.' "

"Have you not ? You had the air of observing her at breakfast."

And to this my lord's eyes answered very intelligibly ;—" then you must have been closely observing me."

"How does the day end here?" he asked, after a short pause. "What I mean is, how do you dispose of the remainder of the day?"

"Why, for the ladies, after dinner, that is, a reasonable time after dinner—the female friends walk together; and for the gentlemen —they join them when they think proper."

"Is that when they feel inclined?"

"I believe it is the same thing."

"Shall you walk after dinner?"

"Oh! I hope so," and the last words brought her to the house door.

In Mrs. Robert Spender's journal of this day—if she had kept a journal, which she did not—would have been found such an entry as the following one—

"In the evening we walked late—I, Julia, and Lord Featherstone—and had a charming conversation."

*   *   *   *   *

Letter from Lord Featherstone to Captain Sullivan.

August 31st.

"Now have you twenty times this day depicted to yourself your friend and his heroine in the moment of the *denouement* of this romance. What visions of a rapturous clearing up of all mysteries has your imagination presented! What shriekings, what faintings, what assurings, what recoverings, what weepings and upbraidings, what acknowledgments and kneelings for pardon, what claspings of hands, what wiping of eyes, what glorifying of Providence and returning arm-in-arm to make known to the select company assembled in the Ll———d Wells boarding-house that 'I, Philip,' and 'I, Julia,' and all the rest of it!

"My good fellow, let your imagination have gone any pace it may, I defy it to have got ahead of the reality. Prepare yourself for such a scene as you have not essayed to depict; one that shall make you look back and laugh with very merriment at your own delineations. Prepare for a surprise.

" We met to-day in the full light of the morning in the drawing-room, she and I alone; every soul of the visitors upon the walk; servants only in the house, and those in another part of it; salts, scents at hand; water no farther off than the table outside the door; all prepared for a scene; and the lady —did not recognise me. By the Lord! I must lay down my pen to laugh at the blankness of your visage, Fred."

Then, Lord Featherstone resumes to give an account of the meeting between himself and the lady, who is the subject of this letter, as it has been already related. " We bowed," he says; " by Jove! yes, we bowed. I afterwards made one of a riding party that included her; and in the evening I walked with her cousin and herself.

" Well, it is a tribute to the cleverness of

my disguise, and I meant it to be a disguise, *n'est-ce pas?* Assuredly a disguise of my person; and in all other than personal respect, I am more than contented that the awkward lover and unfledged *roué* of twenty and not quite one, should be unrecognisable in your friend, sir.

"As for the lady, you have heard me eulogise her beauty, is it not so? I believe it to have been the creation of a love-crazed mind. If otherwise, I defy my own face to be more changed than hers. Changed is the fit word. It is not that she is the wreck of the person she was, she is a different person. For the loss of brilliancy I was prepared; but feature, countenance, air, manner, height! It would be impossible, I think—yet, no! I should have known her.

"After all—another compliment for your friend, my Frederic—she has less the aspect of suffering than I could have expected, notwithstanding this extraordinary alteration. She is singularly calm; but I have watched her, and it is neither the calmness of exhaustion nor of despair. To-night, as we walked, she was evidently pre-occupied. To own the truth, too, her indifference piqued me, and though I addressed myself principally to her cousin, from whose side she made no attempt to withdraw me, I was not unconscious of a wish to engage her attention, and entirely failed to do so. Not that she was silent. She spoke pretty frequently, and took a polite interest in what was said by others; nevertheless there constantly arose an air of being engaged with her own thoughts, distinctly perceptible to me.

"I observed her, also, later in the evening, and believed that the book she held had been taken up only to cover her real occupation. Those thoughts of hers must have been pleasant ones, or the deuce is in it if she would have looked so contentedly in their company. If I were a vain fellow, and a believer in the existence of certain presentiments and sympathies, I should no doubt, be ready to imagine that the proximity of an individual of your acquaintance had diffused over her spirit this inexplicable serenity; a dawn, so to speak, heralding the rising of the great sun of her felicity. What says your philosophy on such a subject ?

" And here, methinks, you ask why I have not discovered myself to the lady ? Certainly it is my purpose to do so; yet, I have not done it. I may take the freak any hour of the day, or—our apartments adjoin—night. I observe her with a sort of contemplative curiosity; meanwhile, my usual good fortune has not deserted me. A young lady, in your style rather than in mine, 'tis true, makes kind eyes at me, and the lively Diana throws herself at my head. Doubtless, things will arrange themselves.

"September 3rd.

"It is a little strange that out of the six persons whom I knew so well formerly there is only one whom I now and then remind of myself. If a whisper to the effect that Philip Vaughan had not so surely died in India, were to reach her ear, my secret would be in danger from Mrs. Fleming. Occasionally I have seen a sudden turn of her head, a quick glance of her eye at some, probably, familiar word, or tone, or look, or gesture of mine recalling for a moment her old admirer. Eleven years have, it must be owned, increased rather than improved her; not, though, to an absolutely disfiguring extent, and she is handsome still. I do not regard it as time altogether misapplied when I take a turn with her on the Pump Walk, or give her my arm as far as the chalybeate spring. If she continue to imbibe the last, it will, I am in-clined to think, occasion her a fit of apoplexy. I imagine, however, the walk, not the water, to be her attraction to the spot, and therefore it remains with me to save her valuable life at any time.

"You have drawn all this upon yourself, and my egotism is in sheer obedience to your commands. I own your position is not an enviable one ; and since you complain that you have only too much leisure (in the early days of September!) for light reading, light reading you shall have. So much am I in the humour for opening my soul into the plenitude of your unoccupied time that one of these first fine—or more probaby, wet— days, I will take my 'grey goose quill' between my fingers, and commit collectedly and systematically to paper the romance of my early life. By the gods! what a romance!

" With this consolatory promise, I remain, my dear Fred Sullivan,

" Yours faithfully,

" FEATHERSTONE."

" Pump House.
    " Ll——d Wells."

CHAPTER IV.

AN EXPEDIENCY.

. . . . . . " And meanwhile," wrote the Earl, some four days after the second date of the letter with which we concluded the last chapter, "meanwhile we have ridings and drivings, and the d——l knows what besides, from morning till night. Idleness is, they say, the mother of mischief, and I have seen no such parent here; yet I more than suspect the existence of the babe. That same prolific lady must, I imagine, have paid the

Wells a visit before my arrival, and left her
infant, which has found protectresses, and
thrives.

"A man might, I fancy, pass half a dozen
days in more refined society than this of the
Ll——d boarding-house, and yet occupy himself less agreeably than I have found it possible to do. Nay, so little heavily has the
time hung upon my hands, that as yet no
vacant ten minutes have presented themselves
in which to discover myself—bah! the word
is not an inspiriting one.   These vacant ten
minutes have, perhaps, not been the more
energetically sought because the enlivening
discovery to which on coming here I destined
them, will uncomfortably interrupt a very
piquante flirtation with—her cousin.

"Nevertheless, I am perfectly alive to the
necessity—expediency is a better word—to
the expediency you speak of. Doubtless, ''twere
well it were done quickly.'   An' I remember
rightly, however, an *if* belongs to the passage
I have in part quoted. By Jupiter! my

Frederic, where eleven years ago were my eyes?
Rather, where was my nicer discernment?
where was my juster appreciation of the attractive qualities of wit, tact, observation, and
the most sparkling and exciting liveliness
(not to mention a strong under current of
passionate feeling of which I am just beginning to suspect the existence) possessed by a
woman who, if I could then read the *sexe* at
all, was not ill-disposed towards myself?
Why is there no Bastille for the sons of gentlemen from seventeen to twenty-five?   Not
years, however, but the events of years, bring
wisdom ; and, to say the truth, the beauty of
Julia might have blunted the edge of a dis-
crimination tempered by even a quarter of a
century's experience of the world.

"She is very beautiful, Fred,—and if
beauty were a woman's greatest possible attraction—Last night, for instance, sitting near
the window in the moonlight, the lovely outline of her features took even me by surprise,
and called up two or three old recollections

D 2

that for the space of perhaps a minute rendered me a somewhat unamusing companion to Mrs. Robert Spender. Charming Diana! Attractive as she is naturally and without effort, I am convinced, if ever I read woman rightly, that she exerts herself to be yet more attractive in my eyes. You will wonder, possibly, how I can enjoy so much of her society among these people; but the merit is not with me. She is, it appears, so recognised a coquette that nothing she can do in that way excites particular attention. In fact, the tone of the society here is not a very rigid one. You may recollect, or more probably you have forgotten, that stern enforcement of an old-fashioned propriety was not the distinguishing feature of the Heath House in former days; and I perceive something of the same *vis-à-vis* to extreme restraint to prevail in this remote Welsh mansion, occupied for the moment by English water drinkers.

"Yet—now, you say, or never; and you say right. You know the resolutions I brought with me to this place were of the most virtuous nature. Still, this finding myself absolutely unrecognised *is* a snare set in the way of a man in my position. *Think* what a field would be now open to my amusement, ay, and to my ambition—but for that one fence! I might leap it, and it would no longer stand in the way of the first; but while it stands at all it is a bar to the second. Fred, in the mind in which I am to-day I would at once and for ever forego all idea of turning resurrection-man to the secrets of the past, did I not fear they might one day disentomb themselves and walk in yet ghastlier grave-clothes into the future. Pleasure and power have not failed to present themselves to my imagination in their most enticing forms; but—but—my Mentor, your Telemaque stands now upon the vantage ground of two-and-thirty years, and from this his comprehensive eye discerns an ugly diverging of the road that might seem from a lower level temptingly direct. To a man who is a

' good hater,' and not forgetful of certain former passages between General Vaughan and himself, it would not be desirable that a nail should be found on which to hook a pretext for disturbing the legitimacy of any future son of his.   Do you perceive?

"For the lady—I believe I have not exchanged a dozen words with her in the last three days.   It must be owned she seems sufficiently satisfied to be neglected, and except her indifference piques me, or I have to remind myself of the necessity of self-command, I forget even her existence.

"I had a riding engagement for this afternoon, which it is my mood to break.   Ten minutes ago, therefore, I sent my regrets, per waiting-maid, to Mrs. Robert Spender's chamber; and now I hear the horses, and will reconnoitre the riding party from behind my villainously scanty curtain.

"They are off! Mrs. Robert Spender looking as little pleased as I could reasonably desire ; the fair Eliza, who really seems now

and then almost a match for Mrs. Spender
herself, in excessively fine feather between
her rival's liege lord and Captain Fleming ;
and Julia, as serene as usual, sitting her
horse, as she always did, more gracefully than
any other woman I ever saw, and certainly
the most insensible to my absence of any of
the party.

" I am undetermined whether to go down
stairs and have a little talk with Mrs. Fleming, or to seize my present writing mood to
enter into the details of a story with the outline of which you are acquainted. I will do
the last. So, dispose yourself to give your
sympathising attention.

" You know, I think, that even for an
embryo man of the world my tender years
were remarkably tough. I was not addicted
—as were some whom I could name—to
leaving my heart with beautiful peasant girls
at cottage doors, or piquante apprentices of
milliners at second story windows, or to ex-
changing locks of hair with little cousins, or

to yearning to become the proprietor, with
' one fair spirit for my minister,' of every
out-of-the-way and ivy-covered tenement
that seemed to offer the minimum of convenience, and the largest number of earwigs.
I was not addicted to those things, and therefore what I am about to relate may seem to
you, as it has often seemed to myself, the more
remarkable.

" It was an afternoon in the May of 182—
that I found myself gazing from the box of a
stage coach, on the features of a wild kind of
unpicturesque country adjacent to the common place—yet rather too desolate and lifeless
looking to be common-place—little market
town of Westbridge.   We had passed over
a couple of miles or so of heath, and were beginning to descend a hill on the side of which
—and incompletely screened by its own
plantation from my elevated eyes—stood a
square brick mansion, commanding an area
of but moderately cultivated land, a few
scattered farms, and the church spire and

chimneys of Westbridge. Between its lodge-gate and the Westbridge turnpike, I observed a somewhat misanthropical looking house—not entitled in any way to be called a place, yet more than a cottage—having an old-fashioned garden between it and the road. Then came the outskirts of the town, and then the town itself. Certainly nothing could be less interesting. Why, then, when the coach stopped to change horses, was I sensible of a most unusual inclination to be left behind? Explain this if you can.

" With or without explanation, I asked if there was fishing in the neighbourhood, and, being told that it was strictly preserved, con-tradiction determined me. My rod, basket, and portmanteau were handed down from the roof, and, standing on the pavement, I watched the coach as it got again into mo-tion, rattled over the stones, and turned the corner of the street. Then I thrust my hands into my jacket pockets, and with grave and remorseful doubts as to the possibility of existing for twenty-four hours within the limits of Westbridge and its environs, walked into the inn bar.

"Notwithstanding that the barmaid was pretty, this same existence was, in fact, a difficult matter. As for fishing, I had never really intended it ; since leave could not be —I was told—readily obtained, it was not, for a few hours, worth while to ask it. In my strolls, evening and morning, I had met, besides the trades, or country, people, but one elderly man of a forbidding aspect; and probably no sounds have ever been greatly more pleasant in my ears than were those of the wheels of the coach that was to take me on my retarded journey.

"It was while I was watching over the welfare of my unused fishing-rod from the window of 'mine inn,' absolutely while folding the bill I had just discharged, into a compass calculated to admit of its entrance into my purse—it was at this moment that my eye happened to fall on the doorway of a linen draper nearly opposite. Now, I had hitherto seen this doorway either empty, or occupied by the shopman, or by two or three country persons, or (but this towards night and lamp-light) by an evident servant girl of the place. It was not to be expected, therefore, that my eye—which, when it wandered in that direction, did so quite involuntarily—should be instantly withdrawn on perceiving something that wore extremely brief petticoats, and possessed unexceptionable ancles, something that was distinctly *not* a servant girl, standing near the counter.

" It appeared the young lady had concluded the business that brought her to the shop, for she had a small parcel in her hand, and a few light drops of rain sufficiently accounted for her continuing to avail herself of shelter, as well as for the next movement of the shopman, who brought forward a chair, which was accepted, to the door, and retired to the back of the premises himself. Now, the unexceptionable ancles advanced a little into the doorway, and I looked at them, the brief petticoats by no means interfering, without let or hindrance; but at the young lady's face, which her position brought exactly into the centre of a pane in the side window, I looked through the glass. Our regards were charmingly mutual; and while I noted that, without being the possessor of unquestionable beauty, she had very remarkably sparkling and intelligent eyes, hair that was cleverly arranged, and a sort of struggling smile, quite otherwise than unbecoming, she could not have remained very ignorant of the handiwork of nature as exemplified in my features. Still, she was extremely demure, and when my eyes became more eloquent, hers were cast upon the ground with a niceness of propriety at which no spinster school-mistress in the three kingdoms could have cavilled.   I descended to the door of the inn, to the pavement ; I put on my gloves; the eyes were inexorable.   I reached the side of the coach ; they vouchsafed not a glance.   I mounted to the roof; the smile was a little more decided, but the eyes as immovably fixed on the point of a very well-fitting boot as before. And now the coach was in movement. It rattled away, and the horn of an amateur resounded through the street.

"We were already at the corner, and I turned to obtain, perhaps, a parting glance from my incognita, who rose in the moment lightly from her chair, and, beholding the helplessness of my position, curtsied to the ground. We were half through the next street before I recovered from my astonishment; and then—conceive, sir, the affronted manhood of twenty years.

"My resolution was taken in an instant. It was taken and it was kept. I went on to the next town, and there hired a horse and and gig, with which I returned to Westbridge."

CHAPTER V.

JULIA.

"A FEW inquiries in the place," continued my Lord Featherstone, "led me to the conclusion that the young lady must be the daughter of a gentleman occupying the house I had remarked a little outside the Westbridge gate; not the mansion at the top of the hill, but the house between that and the turnpike. He was, I learned, a morose, unsocial man, or, at least, looked on as such in the town, where it was believed that his antecedents had been painful ones. Besides this daughter, he had a niece, and though he rarely associated with any one, and never admitted a soul within his doors, the cousins were accounted lively, were a great deal with the family at the Heath House, and walked and rode about the country quite as much—so the landlady informed me—as was good for them.

" With this knowledge of the enemy's position, I set out on a coolish spring evening to reconnoitre the ground between Westbridge and the Heath House.

" My first sortie bid fair for a good while to be an unsuccessful one. On the road I met a sporting looking character, with a brace of dogs, who got over a stile into the plantations I have before mentioned; and I saw the scowling personage I had passed on the previous evening, walking at a quick pace round and round the garden of what I had settled was the habitation of my incognita. He was, therefore, the father and uncle, but no vestige of a daughter or niece could I discern about the premises. I was returning irritated—but not discouraged—to the town, when, at a bend in the road, I beheld the identical persons whom I sought coming towards me from Westbridge. My heart beat quicker. Not that *it* was, in the usual acceptation of the words, concerned in the matter. In addition, however, to the desire for some slight revenge on the fair lady who had been hardy enough to throw after me such a defiance, what I had heard in Westbridge had stirred the spirit of adventure that was to uprise so uncontrollably in after time. I advanced, then, no doubt, triumphantly, and with an expression of countenance that, notwithstanding the self-possession of Diana, brought the bright colour into her cheek. Then my eye turned—simply that I might know it again—on her companion's face.

" I need not say that this was my first meeting with Julia. I did not move—not, I believe, an eye or a finger—till the cousins had passed me by almost half the distance between me and their own home.   Then I turned, and slowly followed them.

" When you see the person who had in a moment of time wrought such a revulsion of feeling in my heart, who had already emptied it of the mixed and trifling motives I had brought with me to the encounter, and im-planted in their room the most ungovernable, the most desperate passion I have ever known, the sight of her will afford you no explanation of the matter.   She is beautiful, unquestionably beautiful, still ; but it is not the beauty of Julia.   You will see a tall and elegant figure, whose elegance is its chief merit.   You will see a face that has the cor-rect outline of some Grecian statue, and a purity and whiteness that assist the resem-blance. You will see eyes as serene as a sum-mer evening sky.   You will see a smile as sweet and tender as if it would pity all the world, and did pity the greater portion of it.

You will see this, but—you will not see Julia.

"Nor can I paint her for you. As well might I try to paint the sunlight—I mean the sunlight *itself*—or laughter, or the sound of the most rippling, ringing little brook that ever danced and dimpled under heaven on a morning in May. Well, I can tell you that she had large eyes, that were intensely blue—that were intense in every respect—in light, in depth, in truth, in trustfulness, and in affection. I can tell you that she had a small, rosy mouth, and soft pink cheeks, and a chin like Venus, and a throat like a Psyche, and a figure like whatsoever is most beautiful in youth, and health, and innocence, and a small foot, and a slender ancle, and folds of soft, fair, shining hair, in which she could wrap herself, when she chose to do so, as in a shawl. I can tell you this, but—mind you— you have not seen Julia.

" To resume. I followed her within a few yards of her own gate, saw her into the house, distinguished her figure and that of her cousin in an upper-chamber. I even remained till candles were brought into a room on the ground floor, and till the shutters were closed. Then I returned to Westbridge.

"I had been told that leave to fish was difficult to obtain, but difficulty now was nothing. I sent my card and a note to the Heath House, and that same night received from Captain Fleming not only the permission I had requested, but a polite invitation to dine at the end of my day's sport. Need I say I accepted it? Need I say I did my possible to propitiate my hostess—a good-hearted soul, in her way, I believe, both then and now? Need I say I was successful? or that, on my mentioning the young ladies I had met near the turnpike-gate, she immediately offered to ask them to dinner if I would repeat *my* visit on the following day?

"We forget sights and sounds, Fred, more easily, I believe, than sensations; and eleven years with all their charms and their changes have not obliterated from my memory the excitement of that next evening. My admiration of Julia as it was excessive and uncontrollable, so also was it undisguised. I had feared a difficulty in the shape of pique on the part of my earliest acquaintance—the eldest cousin; but there was nothing of the sort to encounter. She had perceived at once the impression that Julia's beauty had made on me, and taken her resolution to give me up with a good grace. Indeed, during the only *tête-à-tête* we had that evening, and which scarcely occupied five minutes, she found time to tell me that she had seen at a glance I was going to fall desperately in love with her cousin Julia—that Julia was a little angel—and that she herself would have been excessively jealous only that, happily for all parties, she was at that moment romantic in another quarter. This other quarter was, she afterwards informed me, a certain brother of our host—the very gallant Major, whose acquaintance I have had the pleasure of making in this house; but who was then with his regiment abroad. I may as well say here that *he* seems to be a bachelor still; and why Mrs. Robert Spender is Mrs. Robert Spender remains unexplained.

"As she was not, however, Mrs. Robert Spender at that time, and the gallant Major being, as I have said, abroad, this always charming Diana found leisure, and was free, to make herself generally agreeable. She played sprightly airs on the piano, to which Julia and I, and Mrs. Fleming and a man with large red whiskers, waltzed. She sang sentimental songs (Fred, she sings divinely), while Julia and I, and Mrs. Fleming and the man with large whiskers, conversed. She said clever, deuce-may-care things, at which Julia and I, and Mrs. Fleming and the man with large whiskers, laughed. Her own laugh, clear, and piquante and musical, rang pleasantly out through the drawing-room windows on to the terrace, up and down which Julia and I (and *not* Mrs.

Fleming and the man with large whiskers) strolled, delivering ourselves of such little speeches as were suitable to the occasion and the hour. Finally, a port-folio of her spirited drawings, exposed on a table in a corner, offered the most plausible excuse that could have been desired for my passing the in-door remainder of the evening with the object of my adoration, and to a considerable extent aloof from everyone else. I can easily conceive that the pleasure of the evening derived no small portion of its zest from the presence of the goddess's brilliant namesake. I fear, however, I was ungrateful enough to credit her with little, if any, of the satisfaction I experienced. Even when, towards twelve of the clock, it was my happiness to escort the cousins home, and I permitted myself to be amused by the liveliness of the one, it was to the proximity of the beautiful other that I attributed my willingness to *be* amused.

" I have already carried this letter to an unconscionable length, and will defer proceeding with the subject to another day (or hour), and another sheet. The equestrians will not, I venture to prophecy, extend their ride beyond reasonable limits, and I see Mrs. Fleming on the Pump Walk with only a parasol over her cap. Without a bonnet she will not exhibit herself as far as the chalybeate spring. I may venture, therefore, to join her. Vale !

" FEATHERSTONE."

" Pump House,

    " Ll——d Wells

" September 7th."

CHAPTER VI.

VEXATION.

THE Earl found Mrs. Fleming labouring under unusual excitement. Had he heard that Lady Jones was going to leave the Wells on Friday?

He had not. Would mourning be indispensible?

The jest could have been dispensed with. Mrs. Fleming evidently thought the matter *no* jest. "It is," she said, "most provoking. Lady Jones had fully intended staying another fortnight, which would be about the time our own party and the Spenders proposed to remain. An hour ago, however, just when they were all setting off for their ride, she gave out that her grand friend, the Lady Something Palmer she is always bringing up, had invited her sooner than she expected, and she would not disappoint her dear friend for half a world."

"She will not, however," said the Girl, "carry away the Wells in that prodigious bonnet-box of hers, in which we feel sure there must be so much room to spare."

"Indeed, I don't know! Five minutes after Lady Jones had expressed *her* intentions, the Miss Davies's found that it was getting damp, and the evenings chilly; and I left them each screaming into an ear of poor, deaf old Mr. Morgan, about horses, and coaches, and fees to guards."

"But it may be possible to outlive even this departure. It seems to me that there will be better rooms for some of those who remain."

"Indeed, I don't know!" again said the lady of the Heath House. "Fleming has been worrying to get home ever since the partridge shooting began, and Robert Spender will not stay *after us*."

Lord Featherstone walked on rather thoughtfully.

" And," continued Mrs. Fleming, " the most provoking part of the business is that it is really, to a great extent, your lordship's fault."

"My dear lady !"

" If from all the hours you have devoted every day to Mrs. Robert, you had only spared a few minutes to Lucy Jones, you might have kept her mother here till Christmas."

" Upon my word, you flatter me extremely. But you should have suggested the measure while it might have availed."

" To you ! Excuse me, my lord, but I do

not exactly think you need to see with other people's eyes.   And after all," said the good lady, " after all, as we are on the subject of eyes, your lordship's are such very good ones, that I find it difficult to believe you don't know how to use them.   For instance," and she looked the earl full in the face, " What do you think of Julia ?"

" Of—"

" Of Julia Verity?   Ah, well!   I see I am to hear nothing from you on the subject.   I, at all events, can remember Julia the most beautiful creature that, I believe, ever existed; and adored by a man of whom your lordship so reminds me, that I sometimes wonder— though it seems unlikely—whether he could have been any relation—a Mr. Vaughan ?"

" It is possible," replied his lordship, coldly.

" Perfectly beautiful she was !" said Mrs. Fleming, returning to Julia; "and surely she is very lovely, even now.   While as to Diana —setting apart a certain air and good teeth—

in the name of goodness what loveliness has she ? Wit—good-temper—agreeability—I grant her—but beauty! none."

" I cannot agree with you," answered Lord Featherstone. " But, if it were so, is it not possible that the agreeability you speak of may sometimes be even more captivating than beauty?"

" Yes," replied Mrs. Fleming, " I admit it. Something of the sort, at least, has always been very much my opinion, so I suppose I must be contented to believe that it is yours. There come some of the party; Mrs. Robert, and Julia, and Fleming,—and Eliza, and Robert Spender behind. I shall make it my business to give Miss Eliza a little talking to about that ;—not that it is so much her fault, for he will scarcely lose sight of her for a minute. How they have all kept together."

" But where," said Lord Featherstone, " is Major Fleming? He has deserted."

The riding party could give no account of him. He had ridden off half-an-hour before, suddenly, without a word of explanation to anybody, as fast as his horse's legs could carry him.

Mrs. Robert Spender [suggested that the impending separation from Lady Jones had affected his head, and as an occasional game of *ecarté* with the well dowered widow had already given rise to some mirth at his expense, this suggestion was received with a good deal of laughter. It likewise introduced the subject of departure. This was loudly discussed by the whole party, with the exception of Mrs. Robert herself, who rode a little in advance of the rest, and of my Lord Featherstone, who walked by her side.

"I have been talking to Mrs. Fleming," said the earl, "for the last fifteen minutes; her mind seems made up."

"I expected as much!" Mrs. Robert replied.

"But that will not influence you, or your husband, or your cousin."

"It will influence my husband."

" I hope not."

" I feel sure of it. We shall not outstay the Flemings."

" It is impossible," said his lordship, "that we are to part in this way."

" Sooner or later," Mrs. Robert said, " it must have come."

" And where then," he asked, after a pause, " do you go from here ?"

" We live in Westshire. We shall go home."

" I may very probably visit Westshire; indeed I shall do so. And you will be in London in the spring ?"

" Oh, no !"

" Not in London in the season ?"

" I am afraid not."

Here they were made aware by the exclamations of the persons in the rear that Major Fleming was in sight, and turning they beheld him coming towards them at a gallop. The account he could give of himself was most satisfactory. He had got scent, he said, of an old harper, and had been following it for five miles round the country. He, the old harper, had proved to be only an old fiddler; but the major had secured him, which was the main point. That gallant officer would send his gig and groom to meet him, and he would reach the house by the time tea was over.

"At least," whispered Lord Featherstone, as, having assisted Mrs. Robert from her horse, he pressed the hand he relinquished; "at least we may look forward to some pleasant hours still."

The lady hastily gathered together the folds of her riding-habit, ran upstairs to her own room, and when there burst into tears. Now, as she had usually some flirtation on hand, and was not unaccustomed to allow the presence or absence of her admirers to exercise some influence over her spirits or temper, it never occurred to her to take herself to task for a rather greater amount of agitation than usual. From this circumstance I would attempt to draw the inference that the sort of

flirtations which a certain style of married
ladies are accustomed to account exceedingly
harmless, do at the least a good deal of
initiatory mischief. I would attempt to draw
this inference if I believed any one would be
the better for its being drawn; but as I think
the Mrs. Robert Spenders of society are not
very candid with themselves, and as those
who are not very candid with themselves are
not at all likely to profit by the candour of
others, I will, as the Scotch say, "save my
breath to cauld my parritch."

It did, however, presently occur to the
young married lady in question that her husband, who might be expected upstairs to make
some slight toilette for dinner, would be surprised to find his lively lady weeping; and
that if he should chance to connect together
in his mind the two circumstances of her
tears and her approaching departure from
Ll——d Wells, he might stumble on a conclusion undesirable for all parties. She
washed her eyes, therefore, with rose water,
and proceeded to dishabit herself and dress.

Dinner on that day was, as might be expected, a little dull; Mrs. Robert Spender no longer sparkling, animated, and the gaiety of the table, looked pale and pre-occupied, threw herself back in her chair, ate little, and said less. She derived, it is true, some small consolation from perceiving that my Lord Featherstone was scarcely less pre-occupied than herself. He hardly opened his lips, and followed the ladies from the dining-room.

I will not undertake to say that because Mrs. Robert Spender hastily put on her bonnet and shawl and repaired to the Pump Walk she expected the earl to join her there. I hope she did not expect him to join her there, as, if she did, her disappointment must have been severe. Her walk was uninterrupted, and while she walked his lordship was seated quietly in his bedroom, the window of which afforded him a view of the Pump Terrace, and writing the letter which will be the subject of the three following chapters.

CHAPTER VII.

AN "ILL-OMENED AFFAIR."

"To continue," wrote Lord Featherstone, even with the well-folded cashmere, the light blue silk dress, and the little plain straw bonnet of Mrs. Robert Spender before his eyes, "To continue—Julia and I were soon declared lovers; and, as an instance of the actual ignorance of the world of these two young girls, my declaration was productive of as much pleasure to them as if there had been money, publicity, and the consent of friends to back it. My love was all that Julia thought of, and my proposal, as she termed it, satisfied her cousin.

"It is not easy to say what I proposed to myself at the moment. My love for the woman with whom I had just entered into so important an engagement had, I have since thought, the recklessness without the romance proper to the passion of a boy of my years. The excess of her beauty, the situations in which we constantly found ourselves, the opportunities of the Heath House, all contributed to the increase of my infatuation, and to deter me from serious consideration of consequences. I have fancied that the watchfulness of the cousin who, with not much greater knowledge of the world than Julia herself, had vastly more natural shrewdness, went far to develope, if not to engender, certain evil aspirations. In course of time I began to perceive that her eye and her manner had in them not a little of distrust,—that Julia and I were left together more rarely and for shorter spaces. I need not, however, speak of this. Facts, not feelings, are the things with which I have to do; and Julia was innocence, and unconsciousness, and purity itself.

"It was not till letters from home could no longer be put aside, nor their demands evaded, that I opened my eyes fully to the real state of my feelings in regard to my stay at West-bridge. To make Julia mine! this was my determination, at the least possible cost to myself; but still to make her mine even at any cost.

"The evening of the day on which I received and replied to the latest of the letters of which I have just spoken, I spent at the Heath House, or, rather, in the grounds belonging to it. Julia and I, in right of our engagement, were left much to ourselves; but ever and anon, when the cousin joined us, I perceived an uneasiness in her looks that roused all my anger. I ought not to have been angry. She was a child herself—clever, but still a child, and a well meaning one. In fact, however, Julia in her perfect fearlessness and incomparable simplicity was a thousand times more unapproachable than Diana would have been in Julia's place.

" It is unnecessary to linger over this part of the story. You know the act of insanity which I have never repented but once since I committed it. Yet even there I defended every inch of ground, ay, to the church door. Even at the last moment I clung to the belief that under all the unusual circumstances of the case, between the privacy of the ceremony, the youth of the parties, the non-sanction of parents, the absence of friends, some informality must be enacted in the marriage. But for the obstinate intervention of Diana (by my soul she owes me some compensation) the parson would have been of my providing. As my ill-stars, however, would have it, she numbered amongst her admirers a young clerical nincompoop, doing duty for an absent incumbent in a thickly peopled

parish of a certain manufacturing town remote from Westbridge. This fellow would,
she averred, for love of her bright eyes,
marry, without any unnecessary investigation
or publicity, Julia and myself. It became my
private opinion, on making the acquaintance
of one of the very loosest fish it has been my
fortune to discover in (so-called) holy orders,
that he would have read the service over
Satan for a five pound note. This, however,
is beside the matter. The remote manufacturing town was not inaccessible. It was the
annual privilege of the cousins to leave home
during four or five summer weeks for the re-
freshment of change of air and sea-bathing;
and it was within their ability to substitute
this manufacturing town for one of their ordinary places of resort on the coast. Julia
left everything to Diana, with whom I found
I dared not contest the point. The journey
was made, the banns were published, and one
fine morning in the presence and with the
knowledge only of the reverend performer of

the ceremony, of his pew-opener, candle-lighter, domestic factotum, and gardener (four in one), of the contracting parties themselves, and of Diana, the ill-omened affair took place.

"And here let me pause to ask why in the name of consequences and common sense does not society insist that so important a social contract as marriage shall be cele-brated with greater publicity? Why does not the law provide that the marriage cere-mony shall be performed under circumstances of great publicity, and not otherwise? Don't tell me of difficulties. Men can be got to-gether on other occasions. We have grand juries, and petty juries, and coroners' juries, and common councils, and boards of every-thing under the sun; and why, then, cannot men be assembled officially, responsibly, and in numbers, to witness marriages? Why— not instead of, but in addition to this—should not every parish send up its register monthly, weekly, daily, if it were needful, to be printed and published throughout the length and breadth of the land? I can understand, of course, the sort of objections that might be urged, the sort of evil that might be apprehended; but to my mind and in the light of my own experience, 1 can see no evil so great as those liable to result from a questionable or a concealed marriage. I must give them a turn at this some fine day in the House of Peers.

"In something less than a week from the morning I became a bridegroom I received a letter from my mother. It contained the news of the engagement of my eldest sister to a man whom I know they had been moving heaven and earth to secure for her almost ever since she entered her teens. It likewise conveyed the general desire of the family, and my father's permission, for the postponement for some further time of my return to ———, and an invitation to be present at the wedding. My mother's letter was a long one ; and at the same time that she inquired rather minutely into the attractions of Westbridge, and hazarded a few seemingly chance remarks on the inexpediency of boyish entanglements in any obscure quarter, she took the occasion which Olympia's brilliant marriage offered, to express how much it was her hope that all her children might select their future fates with equal prudence. She addressed herself—she said—particularly to *me;* and was at the trouble of explaining, on something more than half a sheet of paper, that a girl might in some cases be held excusable for according acceptance to an exceptionable *parti,* rather than risk remaining single, but that for a man there could be no such apology. It cannot be said that my mother's letter opened my eyes to the folly I had enacted, since they had only been wilfully and consciously and for the moment closed; but it certainly held a light to that folly by which it looked like an act of madness. Concealment, and to escape from Westbridge, were perhaps the first idea and the first impulse that presented themselves. At this distance of years I forget how I accounted to Julia for abridging even the very short period of time she had expected me to pass with her. The very circumstance of our earlier separation served admirably to excuse the ill humour which my embarrassment and, already, my remorse had engendered, and which I could not perfectly control. The incense Julia's grief offered to my vanity diminished, no doubt, the bitterness I carried to the interview; but so little could I, on the appearance of Diana, suppress the remainder, that she, on her part, suffered some uneasiness to appear. She made inquiries respecting my letter—my journey—my family—my home—with more particularity than she had ever done before. I even remarked to her that she appeared dissatisfied. 'Nay!' she replied, 'I satisfy myself in the belief that you stay with Julia the very longest that you can stay.' An evil conscience rendered me ready to imagine that in this a reproach was intended, and I should probably have rejoined with asperity had I not perceived tears in her eyes. If not touched, I had at least the grace to be silenced by the warmth and disinterestedness of her friendship for her cousin.

"My visit to the house of feasting was not calculated to reconcile me to the step I had just taken. A large party of relations had already assembled round Olympia in prepara- for her wedding, and my ears were solaced with infinite repetition of the words 'prospects' and 'pretensions;' not inspiriting ones to a man sufficiently conscious of having just se- curely placed an extinguisher on the first, and rendered the last of no avail.

"Presently the relatives of the bridegroom (such of them as thought fit to add lustre to the affair) began to arrive, and amongst the more remote of these was a lady whose air of distinction struck me in the first hour I spent in her society. This was Lady Carysbrook. Her lord was also of the party; and, notwith- standing that I had been taught to entertain rather lofty notions of the position of my mother and sisters in the fashionable world, it appeared to my growing intelligence our visitors belonged to a grade removed—·I could not have said how—from our own. I perceived that while my mother and sisters and their friends were perfectly at their ease with the calm, cheerful, kindly-mannered Lady Carysbrook, she was not always absolutely unembarrassed by them. I remarked that she accorded the most of her notice to the quietest and most retiring of my sisters. I do not suppose that bashfulness was the charm that attracted her attention to myself, yet she certainly condescended to include me in the notice she took of Ellen, and permitted an occasional attendance on my part such as no other *young* man in the house presumed to offer. Probably my *desire* to please her was not disregarded, and inclined her to think better of me than I merited. I was not without tact even at that early period, and I think she found herself so little delighted by the strangers with whom her kinsman's marriage was about to connect her, that it was a relief to be able to discharge what she might consider necessary civilities to the immediate relations of the bride, in the form of kindness to me. However this might have been, I received, on the departure of the earl and herself, an invitation to meet the newly-married pair at Carysbrook in the ensuing month.

"I discovered, as I expected to do, something very different in the circle assembled at Carysbrook from that which had lately separated at our own house. Olympia and her husband had not arrived, and, to own the truth, having no acquaintance with a soul beyond my host and hostess, I found myself, in so large a party, a good deal overlooked. I had little to do but observe and listen to others, and I desired to recommend myself by my modesty to Lady Carysbrook. The men were chiefly men advanced in years ; the ladies almost all, I imagined, married ; and with more than one face there I was acquainted through the medium of the public prints.

" At my first dinner there sat immediately opposite me one of the only two young women present; and even she, I perceived, wore a wedding-ring. She was extremely beautiful: dark, lively, clever, yet absolutely void of the flippancy that I remembered in my sisters. At a greater distance, and next an elderly, but, it appeared, infinitely agreeable man, sat the person nearest her own age—a girl in her first youth ; and towards her I found myself frequently directing my eyes, not only because I beheld in her a beauty and an air well inviting attention, but because I discovered that she was likewise regarding me. She was exceedingly fair, and possessed delicate features; but what struck me most was that air, indicative, I imagined, of high birth and breeding, which had first attracted me in Lady Carysbrook, and which distinguished my lady and this younger person even here, where all probably were highly born and bred. A resemblance, in other respects than this, induced me to suppose they were related, and I was not mistaken. The young girl was Lady Susan Corfe.

" In the position of this last I found, on further acquaintance, something to surprise me. I at first believed her to be exceedingly what I had heard my sisters call ' kept back;' but on further observation I perceived the contrary. She was evidently less under the espionage of Lady Carysbrook or any other person than I had been accustomed to see young ladies under that of their respective *chaperones*, and the countess, notwithstanding her affection for her daughter, interfered in regard to her to a much smaller extent than her youth seemed to warrant. My surprise was increased by the subsequent discovery that my lord and my lady had no son, and that the Lady Susan was their only child,—a position so splendid in my eyes that I was lost in astonishment at beholding that, of the nu-

merous party in the house, not a man testified
any desire of recommending himself to her
especial favour.

"Does this narrative of trifles weary you,
my Frederic? Does it appear ludicrous to
you, sir? Trifles at this time had much influence in disposing my mind towards the
course of conduct I afterwards pursued. I
remember to this moment the sort of giddi-
ness that seized me when, in learning the
position of the girl whose chief companion I
had been for several days, there flashed upon
me all she had it in her power to confer.
Bitterly, when I retired to my own room, did
I curse the infatuation which had just united
me in a manner so destructive of all a man's
better prospects ! Had I, indeed, been *free*,
I should not have found the vanity to look for
one moment to a possibility so dazzling, so
beyond my pretensions, as that of 'achieving
greatness' by means of this fair daughter of
Lord Carysbrook ; but—being bound—it
seemed, in the delirium my fetters caused me,

that but for them I might well have aspired to the hand of Lady Susan Corfe. I was a mere lad, sick to death of conquest I had learned to look on as defeat; and the favour I fancied I had found with both daughter and mother, while it inflated my vanity and the presumption of twenty years, engendered an extreme disgust of my own unlucky marriage, and anger against all concerned in it.

" Continually I found myself contrasting my absent bride with this daughter of prosperity; and, notwithstanding that poor Julia's beauty was of an order which Lady Susan's would not by the most prejudiced person have been said even to approach; notwithstanding I had entertained a very real and ardent passion for the one, while with the other I was not the least in love, the comparison was incessantly to the disadvantage of my unfortunate wife, and contributed greatly to the hardening of my heart against the cause of my most rankling regret. The more aristocratic picture was splendidly framed, and seen always in a light the most enhancing possible. Carysbrook, both within doors and without, its noble park, its luxurious rooms, its owner's table, carriages, retinue, and guests, was a setting that could hardly fail to make more apparent to such eyes as mine the value of the jewel it contained. The *entourage* of the fair Susan was wealth, nobility, respect; and the calm, kindly, unassuming, and un-flushed demeanour of one so very highly placed obtained from me far greater admiration than it merited. I overlooked the fact that this young girl had been born where she was, bred where she was. The very simplicity of her tastes, evidencing a poverty of imagination I should now despise, seemed to me at that time philosophical, a thing to marvel at; and the natural eloquence and graceful enthusiasm of Julia became ill-bred, com·pared with the habitually undemonstrative gentleness of Lord Carysbrook's daughter.

CHAPTER VIII.

A COUSIN.

"One day," continued Lord Featherstone, "I had conveyed the spleen and irritability engendered by the position in which I found myself into one of the least frequented of the lovely walks in the vicinity of the house. I had passed the morning beside Lady Susan's work-table, and was absent from her now only because visitors were expected. Ordinary visitors came and went, and those not immediately interested in them knew

nothing beforehand of their arrival or departure. These, however, were not ordinary
visitors, but persons who seemed to be
expected with great pleasure, and even, as
far as such a thing was possible at Carysbrook,
with excitement. At luncheon I heard my
lady express an intention of remaining within
to receive her sister and nephew, and, when
luncheon was over, she and Lady Susan retired
together to their apartments.

"I cursed the expected visitors in my
heart, for I was conscious that I had suffered
more bitterness to escape me in a conversation
I had lately held with Lady Susan than I
could at all have desired to betray, and wished
quickly to efface the ill impression. There
had not appeared in her manner the faintest
appreciation of the cause or aim of my
perversity; but I keenly felt I had said
enough to expose me to the ridicule of a
person possessing more penetration than
herself. In the mood in which I was, a man
could not well have had worse companions

than his own thoughts; yet I rather sourly, as I remember, rejected Olympia's invitation to ride that afternoon with her, and betook myself to a part of the grounds unfrequented, as I have said, but too little remote from sight, if not sound, of the wealth, the prosperity, the enjoyment that was both irritating and deepening the secret sore I carried in my heart. These, bathed in the beautifying sunshine of a glorious summer day, made darker and more cheerless the 'winter of discontent' begun in my own mind. On that afternoon became—I have since believed—imperfectly outlined the plan for the surmounting of my difficulties which I afterwards followed out. I pondered on one spot—the margin of a lake whose extreme elegance of invention had arrested my steps—so long that hours went unregarded by; and assuredly my thoughts were not of a tender, or imaginative, or poetical complexion. The sun during my reverie had made such progress towards the west that I even feared I might miss the dressing-bell, and, anxious to regain the hall, I took a short path to that side of it in which the suite of rooms occupied by the family in private were situated.

" I repented my haste when, emerging from the trees on a terrace that fronted this part of the house, I beheld Lady Susan and another person walking slowly before me. I paused but a moment to observe more particularly the figure of the stranger, which had an attitude that arrested my memory; but in that moment Lady Susan, turning, perceived me, and nothing remained but to walk forward to meet her. A glance at her companion filled up the measure of my annoyance. The nephew of Lady Carysbrook was my old Harrow enemy, Montresor.

" We met—he and I—coldly ; but the surprise, the constraint, the discomposure, were all on my side. I believe I must have made an extremely ridiculous figure in the explanation I endeavoured to offer, for it increased my vexation to discover that the long windows of

apartments I had never been in opened on to
this terrace, and that several of them were
unclosed.   Lady Susan, with her accustomed
sweetness, smiled on my apologies, and pointed
out to me the beauties of the landscape, as
seen from that end of the house.   Her companion said little, but both turned to
accompany me to a door giving admittance
to a passage that communicated with the
principal staircase whence, in no enviable
frame of mind, I made my way to my own
room.   I had certainly never up to that time
suffered so great and so distasteful a surprise.
I had known at Harrow that this Montresor was a fellow born to high fortunes,
and had even then bitterly hated him for the
same ; but I had *not* known that he was thus
nearly connected with such people as the
Carysbrooks, and following on this surprise
came much that I had heard of him from time
to time since we parted.   Though only three
years older than myself, he had already pur-
chased his troop in the —— Life-guards, and

was the author of certain ' Letters from St. Petersburgh,' that had made him a literary name. The immediate augmentation of my hatred towards him was, I think, sir, to be held excusable if we estimate the contrast offered by his present, past, and future, to my own. Now did I at last in unmitigated earnest, by bell, book and candle, by my ambitious aspirations, and by my blighted life, curse my marriage. Hitherto the beauty and goodness of Julia had risen again and again to the surface of sufficiently bitter waters; but after this meeting with Montresor they rose no more.

" I was, however, at Carysbrook, and the dressing-bell had rung. I made my toilette therefore, and for the first pleasurable sensation I had experienced that day I was indebted to .boyish appreciation of my own good looks. On the ground of personal appearance I did not fear even Montresor, and standing before a looking-glass, and reminding myself of the cousinship, and of the unsensational character of the intercourse that had probably subsisted from childhood, I became restored to some requisite degree of self-complacency.

"In descending to the drawing-room I arranged with my own mind to make some advances towards a greater cordiality with Montresor. I hoped, too, to have the opportunity of saying such six words to Lady Susan as might efface the impression possibly left by my ill-humour of the morning. Montresor, however, though already in the room when I entered it, was conversing with Lord Carysbrook and some older men of the party; and the Lady Susan made her appearance almost in the same moment that dinner was announced, in the company of a lady whom I perceived to be her aunt. How irksome to me was that dinner! Nevertheless, since I chanced to sit next an old lord who had rather a caprice for me, I was sufficiently agreeable to him to have the satisfaction of perceiving that I more than once drew the notice of Montresor and others on myself. He—Montresor—said but little during dinner; yet, when the ladies had withdrawn, resisted not some attempts to draw him out, and then did I become still more helplessly the prey of that spleen over which I had to some extent and for a brief period, gained a victory. Happily, he did not tax my endurance long. He rose with the first movement made to leave the dining-room, and was closely followed by me.   Lady Susan and her friend Lady Flora Heathcote sate together.   Montresor went to them immediately, and I— Heaven knows why—wanted at the moment presumption to secure myself a like advantage.

" Lingering near one of the windows, I was presently joined by the old lord next whom I sat during dinner.   I affected to have nothing better to do than listen to him, but in reality I was closely watching, and with an anxiety which became soon converted into astonishment and indignation, the group com-

posed of Montresor, Lady Susan, and her
friend. It was, in the first place, the countenance of Lady Flora that guided my jealousy
to the others. I discovered in her sparkling
eyes a significance of expression that did not
appear to embarrass her companions. After
a while she left them, and Montresor assu-
ming her place, it was with difficulty I could
maintain sufficiently my conversation with the
old peer to prevent his remarking the quarter
to which my observation was directed. In
the end, the flirtation—as I deemed it—between the cousins became to my angry eyes
so unequivocal that I no longer regarded
what was addressed to me. 'Ha !' I exclaimed, as some trifling *petit soin* on the
part of Montresor carried away my last
fragment of composure, 'the life-guardsman
is making the most of his time with the
heiress ! And, by Jove! as it appears, to her
satisfaction.' The old lord looked up at me
in surprise. I repeated the first part of what
I had already said, or to the same effect,

and laughed, I remember, scornfully and loud, my old peer looking more and more astontonished.

" ' Do you not know,' he said, ' that Lady Susan is betrothed to her cousin ?   It is a marriage that has been desired by the parents for years, and by themselves ever since they became old enough to be acquainted with the wishes of their families. You are perhaps surprised that Lord and Lady Carysbrook give their daughter to a commoner, and it is, in fact, a great match for Harry. But he has always been loved by them like a son, and is the representative of a very ancient and wealthy family ; while equally with Lady Susan he is the grandson of a Duke. His predilection for the army has been the cause of a little delay ; but they will be married very shortly now.'

" Thus ran on the old nobleman, and he might have talked for half-an-hour on the matter—possibly he did so—without any chance of interruption from me. ' Do you not know that she is betrothed to her cousin?' were the words remaining the whole time in my ears. All else was for some moments a confusion as of Babel. Nor were my eyes less sensible of the shock I had received. Every object in the room—the men and the women, the satins and the silks, the flowers, the furniture, the lights—even to the brown moustache of Montresor and the rose-coloured robe of Lady Susan, took an aspect that was vague and unsubstantial as things painted on a curtain that some draught of air is moving to and fro. The very floor wavered beneath my feet.

"How that evening passed I cannot easily recall. I have a dim remembrance of affecting to occupy myself with a portfolio of prints. That my mortification was absolutely unperceived—absolutely unsuspected, should have been some consolation; but there was extreme bitterness, as you will guess, even in this. My most prominent consciousness was of an intense desire to be gone from Carysbrook; and hatred of everything, animate and inanimate, within its walls.

" At last I found myself in my own apartment for the night; and opened my pocket-book, and took from it that letter of my mother's that I had received at Westbridge. I read it deliberately through; I paused upon every line; I returned to particular passages. My motive in doing this must have been to strengthen my own purposes. Why else had I kept—why did I now open and read such a letter ? Yet, notwithstanding this, something within me uprose against its worldliness. Such heart—such manhood as I had, half threatened to assert themselves. I folded it— the letter—and I replaced it, and, Fred, a better angel than usually inspires me glided to my side as I folded it. ' Go,' this serene and tender vision seemed to whisper, ' to Lady Carysbrook,—to a woman unacquainted with the narrow views, the devious paths, the un-just aspirations of those walking painfully along a lower level. Go to Lady Carsybrook,

—throw yourself on her compassion and take her counsel.' Why didn't I do this, sir? Why didn't I go to Lady Carysbrook, and throw myself on her compassion and take her counsel? She would have said ' Boy! this modern desire of male youth for money— rather for the fancied ease and false security that money gives—is an evil thing, and will lead to more evil than is just now foreseen. How can you expect us women,' and here she would have smiled her sweet, gracious smile, ' to go forward with uprightness and courage on the battle field of life, if you men creep into the nearest trenches? The young girl is beautiful? is innocent? and loves you? Then count yourself happy. Take her on your arm; confess the act of disobedience to your parents ; avow the act of unworldliness to the world. Lay hold on a profession ; rely on your God, your own exertions, and your friends; and reach the proud platform of well-won distinction.' This Lady Cary-brook would have said, and her words might have counteracted the evil in my mother's letter—might have counteracted the evil in my own heart. But no! I sent my guardian angel to the deuce, remained just long enough at Carysbrook to complete the ill-impression of myself that I was to leave behind me, and then turned my back on it and all that it contained for ever.

" We are ready enough, sir, to attribute our evil inspirations to the devil. Pray where do our good ones come from? My word!—as McPherson used to say—but just for once, and on grounds simply logical and philosophical, I have a great mind to read the Bible.

" I have run my letter to a length neither very merciful to you or to myself, as a gentle aching of my wrist reminds me; yet having pursued this retrospect so far, I am desirous to carry it on to a conclusion, and have done with it—the rather as I fancy I shall scarcely be able in the evening to resume my pen. The people below meditate hilarity. I discover no extraordinary cheerfulness amongst them, but it seems Major Fleming has been riding frantically about the country to procure a fiddler for the ladies, and having found one, I conclude they have no alternative but to dance.

CHAPTER IX.

A DEPARTURE.

" IN conclusion," wrote the Earl, " I returned from this infernal Carysbrook visit to encounter all the questionings of a family party at home.   This, with Oxford in the prospect, and, to vary my *agrémens* in the country, the tenderest letters from my wife, was a state of things not likely to beguile me of the bitterness of my mood. Julia, too, though she forbore to press the declaration of our marriage, urged me to pay her a short visit.   She believed that between my arrival at Oxford and my departure from my father's house I might command a few days; and rather to prevent any suspicions of foul play in the mind of her cousin than influenced by tenderness or even compassion for herself, I promised to spend a few *hours* at Westbridge. Figure to yourself my surprise when I beheld a face pale and careworn; a form emaciated; a smile the light of which only rendered more visible her anxiety, disappointment, and suffering.   Nothing in her letters had taught me to expect the alteration.   Figure to yourself, I say, my surprise,—surprise in the first instant; figure to yourself my horror in the second. There could be but one reason for such a change, and I, Fred, had already ceased to regard her as a wife.

" She must have perceived the shock I had sustained, for such spirits as she brought to the interview forsook her, and one more unsatisfactory can hardly be imagined.   In the same moment that I comprehended there was the birth of a child to be provided for and concealed, I comprehended that Diana was the person with whom I must speak upon the subject. It would not be very easy to do justice to the conduct of the latter. Never, without infringement of delicacy, was a young girl, I should think, so equal to such an occasion; honest warmth of feeling for her cousin and contempt for all affectations, characterised her throughout the affair.

" For myself, my mind was made up. From Oxford I wrote to my father, strongly insisting on my unfitness for the church, and entreating him as he valued my happiness or wished well to my prospects, to interest himself to obtain me a commission in the army. Nay, I particularised; it was a regiment in India I was desirous of entering. My father, I have reason to believe, suspected some entanglement—mark me, he did not suspect, could not have suspected its nature—and, in the end, realised my wishes. Within four months my appointment to an ensigncy in the ——th appeared in the Gazette.

"And in the meantime the desperate illness of Julia had nearly released me from all the embarrassment consequent on my imprudence. The means at my disposal had been limited enough, yet I believed—and believe—that no part of my arrangements were responsible for her sufferings. In the first accounts I received from Diana the child was not expected to live, and for weeks it was supposed that the illness of the mother could have but one termination.

"Nevertheless, both recovered; and the former was removed as soon as practicable by the woman designed to have the charge of it; removed, Julia and her cousin thought, to accompany me to India till such time as I should find myself in a position to return to England, confront my family, and acknowledge the whole transaction. You will not marvel that I pass quickly over this part of my narrative.

The child was of extraordinary beauty, and my heart smote me more for my abandonment of it than for the worst of my conduct to its mother. If ' our sins have thorns wherewith to pierce us,' mark me, Fred! it is by that child I shall be made to bleed.

" To shorten my story, I had no intention of ever beholding Julia again, or of redeeming one of my promises to her. I was quitting England, if not for ever, at least for many years, till all traces of me should have disappeared from the sight of those by whom I only desired to be forgotten, and till I should have formed ties subversive of the ones that bound me there. I need hardly tell you that no word of the army had been suffered to reach Julia or her cousin. They supposed me destined to a merchant's house. I, therefore, obtained a sum of money—at a very heavy sacrifice, God knows—sufficient to indemnify, in that way, a person—not the woman already spoken of—a person who undertook for my sake to supervise the

present, and care for the future, of the child.
She—this person—was conscientious,—that I
knew; and in her own class of life not less to
be respected than even Julia herself. Though
my heart reproached me, then, I satisfied
my conscience, and bade 'my native land,
good-night.'

"A few words more and I have done. They
are scarcely needed. Yours was the pen that
conveyed to Diana intelligence of my death
and that of the child from cholera, then really
raging throughout the part of India to which
they had supposed me destined. From the
hour in which I sealed that letter I gave to
the winds all thought connected with the
ill-starred marriage I imagined dissolved for
ever, and you can, I think, bear witness that
no man could well be less troubled with vain
remorse or weak forebodings. In fine, Julia
was to me but a recollection, the drama of
my past life as a 'tale that is told.' How in
those years of penniless gaiety, of dissipation
and of debt, could it enter my head to imagine

that to me—a soldier of fortune—little better than forgotten by my friends at home, with no apparent future save such a one as I might carve out for myself, and a present income that, crippled as it had been, exceeded only by the paltriest sum, my pay; how, I say, could it enter my head to imagine that to me a wife and son would one day be important pieces in a very different game of life already preparing itself for my hand.   Relative after relative died, and I either heard nothing of their deaths, or dreamed not how nearly their deaths affected me. It was not till I stood next in succession to the earldom that now is mine, that letters from my mother and sisters, who seemed to have themselves suddenly awakened to an appreciation of my consequence, acquainted me with my position; and, as you know, events followed so fast upon each other that ere even my trifling preparations for leaving India were completed, I was a peer. I am interrupted, but half-a-dozen lines will now conclude this letter.   From the moment in which I was able to realise the fact that the coronet of my remote ancestors had descended on my head, I comprehended that the Julia of my early romance must be the Lady Featherstone of my future career. No longer obscure myself, no obscurity must hang over a matter so important as my marriage. That cursed bell is ringing as if twenty fiends were pulling it! I will, perhaps, add a postcript to my letter at night, but in case I do not, here subscribe myself,

"Yours, Fred, faithfully,

"FEATHERSTONE."

CHAPTER X.

WHO CAN HE BE?

I HOPE the old blind fiddler has not been forgotten by the reader. That he had not been forgotten by the company was indicated both by the unaccustomed ascent of the majority of the ladies to their toilet-tables at the conclusion of tea, and by the immediate activity, in the way of preparation, of Major Fleming, who would naturally be master of the ceremonies on an occasion all the credit of which was due to himself. I should not have said the majority of the ladies. Mrs. Robert Spender ascended the stairs, so did Mrs. Fleming, so did Miss Eliza Smith. But Lady Jones and her daughter, and the Misses Davis, followed by old Mrs. Morgan, entered the drawing-room and grouped themselves round the evening fire; and Miss Verity, followed— but of this she was unconscious—by my Lord Featherstone, entered it also, and seated herself near the window, separated from the fireplace by the length of the room. It was not till she had seated herself that she beheld Lord Featherstone bringing a chair to her side, and of course, she turned to him directly.

"This is very sad news, Miss Verity!" he said.

"It is, indeed!—the going away, you mean?" Nevertheless, she spoke so cheerfully that his lordship did not immediately reply.

"I am afraid to say how sad I think it!" he observed, after a short pause, and without lifting his eyes to hers, which he might naturally think were expressing some surprise.

"It is not much more than a week since I first saw you," he resumed, still without meeting her astonished regards. The serenity of her voice, however, was, he found, perceptibly disturbed as she answered—

"No! not much more."

"And since my great and growing admiration for you has been entertained at a distance, my position is a most delicate one; a most difficult one, unless you——"

Here he did lift his eyes, met for a single moment the startled ones of his companion, and beheld a crimson blush rise rapidly over her temples and fair forehead almost to the division of her hair. A blush, however, is not always the most legible character in the world. It may be a blush of anger, or pleasure, or pain, or extreme embarrassment, or unmixed surprise. The pale young lady's blush, then, was no answer to Lord Featherstone, and he spoke again.

"My mind," he said, and in a still lower tone, for the *tête-à-tête* had begun to attract the attention of the persons surrounding the fire; "my mind is made up. I cannot expect—cannot hope that yours will be so here."

"It is quite!" she said as audibly as the position permitted her to speak. Yet his lordship continued as if he had not heard her.

"I cannot ask that yours should be so here. I do not ask it. What I do ask—and I commit my precipitation to your mercy—what I do ask is to be allowed to follow you wherever you may be going, and there prosecute my suit."

With the last words he rose. The eagerness of the voice, however, of the person he had been addressing, its earnest, unmistakable sincerity, detained him in the act of quitting her.

"Lord Featherstone," she said, "I cannot allow you to renew this subject *any* where. Forgive me!—I really feel I have nothing with which to reproach myself."

It was now my lord's turn to colour, and he did so very deeply, standing for perhaps three quarters of a minute with head a little bent beside her. " Nothing !" he then answered in a tone and with an air of profound submission, and turned away, but not till he had flashed upon her a look more legible than a blush ;—a look that completed the unpleasantness of this extraordinary scene, and which (though she beheld him almost immediately chatting and laughing with Mrs. Robert Spender in the passage, and a very little later stood opposite him and the same lady in the first quadrille of the evening) she could not for some time entirely cease to remember.

Lord Featherstone had not, it will be remembered, observed any extraordinary disposition on the part of the company for the amusement Major Fleming had been at so much pains to provide. He—the Earl—had not predicted a success, and the ball was, in fact, a failure. The old fiddler scraped away lustily at every sprightly tune in succession with which he had been accustomed to inspire the feet of bidden guests at weddings half the country round for the last fifty years; but the dancers, or those who should have been such, would not be sprightly. The gallant endeavours of the Major to prevail on Lady Jones to be led out to the absurdest tunes, and the leaps and bounds and steps he executed in his grave attempts to keep something like pace with the spirited performance of the youngest Miss Davis, elicited a good deal of laughter; but then it was laughter of a satirical and unhealthy character, I fear. As for waltzes, they were not, as may indeed be supposed, the old fiddler's *forte;* and a still more serious hindrance presented itself in a deficiency of waltzers. When Major Fleming had with some ingenuity and an invincible good humour fixed upon a tune of the fiddler's that " might be waltzed to," it became apparent that he and his nephew, and Lord Featherstone and Mrs. Robert Spender, made the only two couples available for the occasion. Mrs. Fleming might not perhaps have refused to stand up under other circumstances than those that included Lady Jones as spectatress ; but for the rest of the party—these were, as I have already said, days when Lord Byron was still quoted, and when there were young ladies who "did not waltz." Miss Jones "did not waltz ;" Miss Verity "did not waltz;" Miss Eliza Smith had weak ancles and could not waltz; Captain Fleming was gone to bed ; and Mr. Robert Spender protested inability to turn round to save his soul.

In the end—it came to this. The country dances and tunes that " might be waltzed to " were gradually exchanged by the old fiddler for ditties still more after his own heart ; and while Lady Jones sat up and condescended to approbation, and Mrs. Fleming did her best to be delighted with very dolorous versions of " The Rising of the Lark," and " Poor Marianne," the younger persons drew together in little groups. And when dancing had been altogether given up, the evening improved. Nay, it improved to such an extent that ten

o'clock—the hour of rigorous retirement—
found the company unwilling to separate. It
might be that the harmonies of the old fiddler
had entered with softening influence into the
soul of Lady Jones; it might be that the state
of mind and countenance in which she was
wont to appear at the house of her friend was
already commencing to make itself seen ; it
might be that the *petits soins* of the Major, in
drawing to a close, were also beginning to be
more valued;—from whatever cause, that
officer's gallant entreaty to be permitted to
offer to her and the others of the party negus
and biscuits in the drawing-room was quite
graciously acceded to. Mrs. Robert Spender,
her cousin, and Lord Featherstone, sitting together, and of course included in the invitation, were the last to adjourn. The former of
these, in passing the window, stopped, and
suddenly threw it open—wide. It must be
owned the atmosphere of the room was a little
cloudy, a little close.

"What a lovely night!" she said.

"What a pleasure," added the Earl at her elbow, "to avail ourselves of it! Do you want negus?"

"Do I? Good gracious—no!"

"What does Miss Verity say?"

"Oh, Julia," quickly rejoined Mrs. Robert, "will play propriety, I am certain. I will rush upstairs for our bonnets, and join you in less than half a minute."

In fact she reappeared almost immediately, and the trio proceeded to the Pump Walk. When they gained it Lord Featherstone placed himself between the two cousins, and gave an arm to each.

It was a delicious evening; there was a charming novelty in promenading at such an unusual hour, and the Earl had never been more agreeable. Nevertheless, after a few turns, Mrs. Robert Spender's share in the conversation became gradually less. Her vanity was susceptible. I say *vanity*, because as she was a married lady, it is not fair to assume that more than her vanity could have an interest in Lord Featherstone. Besides, her vanity *was* susceptible—I am perfectly safe in asserting that; and after a while (during which she was too exactly where she liked to be, to feel extremely critical) she began to find an equality in his lordship's tone to herself and to the cousin who was only there to " play propriety," that did not altogether satisfy her. She considered she had a right to look upon the Earl as her admirer, and he should have marked the difference between the lady who was on his arm because he admired her, and the lady who enjoyed a similar position only because she was a cousin of the lady he admired, by a distinction of air, manner, voice—of course, imperceptible (at least, politely imperceptible), to Julia, but perceptible to her. And this her ear, which had considerable acuteness in such matters, did not quite discover. Now, by day, looks might have answered all her demands; but at this hour his lordship might have looked volumes and she been none the wiser or better satisfied. No doubt he was looking volumes, yet when she wished to ascertain it, his head was sometimes turned in a contrary direction; and on these occasions she more than once found herself regarding the figure of her cousin with an appreciation she had not bestowed on it for years. In a light that was far too imperfect to reveal her own attractions of piquancy and variety of expression, she felt almost envious of the elegant height of her cousin, approximating, as it did, so much more nearly to that of Lord Featherstone, while to her naturally just and now jealous ear, Julia's soft musical voice seemed a thousand times better suited to the scene than her own more lively, and on this particular evening, rather querulous tones. The Earl was amusing, unconstrained, and attentive to her. She would have found it difficult to reasonably account for her dissatisfaction. Nevertheless, her share in the conversation became less and less sustained, she was the first to discover that the night had grown chilly, and to suggest the propriety of returning to the house.

"If you suffer," he said. "Otherwise, I would plead for a few minutes more. It may be long before we meet again."

Mrs. Robert remaining silent—rather painfully silent, her cousin thought—the latter gently, and by a gracious, graceful impulse, not to be misunderstood, rejoined—

"Let us hope better things."

They were really the most common-place, almost necessary words, yet Mrs. Robert was sensible of a check, nearly a pause, on the part of Lord Featherstone while they were being pronounced. She was also extremely sensible of the tone of gratification in which he, after the said little check, rejoined—

"Then we will hope better things!" stepping out with a sort of contentment that Mrs. Robert did not think exactly called for. The jealous pang was, however, as shortlived as it was painful, for the Earl's words were scarcely uttered when his steps were again arrested, and the attention of the little party was aroused by the sound of carriage wheels approaching on the road below; a sound so unexpected and unusual at that time of night that the three persons simultaneously halted to satisfy their ears of the reality of the noise before even an ejaculation of surprise passed their lips.

" A carriage!" said the Earl, and he again moved forward. " Who can it bring at this season ?"

" And," exclaimed Mrs. Robert, " at such an hour of the night! Why, we happen to be a little later than usual, or the whole house would have been in bed."

" I cannot say I envy them," rejoined his lordship, " whoever they are. They may have choice enough of rooms, however, in a day or two—supposing them fastidious."

" Choice enough, indeed! Fancy the wretchedness of a party of perhaps only two or three persons in an empty house— miserable !"

"I doubt," said Lord Featherstone, gazing keenly at the carriage as it rolled past them on the road beneath, but without lamps, and imperfectly visible through the straggling trees that interposed. "I doubt if there are even so many as two or three. It is a post-chaise, and not heavily loaded."

Indeed by the time our little party had reached the end of the walk nearest the house, and which commanded a view of the whole front, the chaise had stopped at the door, the people of the house came flocking out, and by the candles brought to receive the visitors both Lord Featherstone and his companions perceived a gentleman alight from the vehicle and enter the passage. A single portmanteau followed him. Then the chaise was slowly turned, and taken round into the stable-yard.

"Humph! a man!" said Mrs. Robert, "and without belongings." And with the malice engendered by the day's mortification in her heart, she turned to her cousin and said—

"Another chance for the young ladies, Julia!"

Julia either did not hear, or did not care to notice the remark, and when the trio reached the house, passed quickly in, and at once ascended the stairs to her own apartment. Mrs. Robert, on the contrary, turned into the deserted drawing-room, and, followed by Lord Featherstone, drew near the fire, and affected to warm her hands at its expiring embers. The Earl placed himself at the opposite corner of the hearth, and rested his arm upon the chimney-piece, but for some moments without speaking.

"You seem preoccupied," the lady said at last, and—I am sorry to have it to tell—in a tone of pique and even bitterness that it appeared she scarcely attempted to suppress.

I am nearly sure he had not been thinking of her, yet he was immediately equal to the occasion.

"Do you wonder at it?" he replied, without the hesitation of a moment, and meeting

unshrinkingly her eyes. " Is not our Ll——d
acquaintance drawing near a close, and who
can say where or when or how we may meet
again ?"

" Possibly never! But you will easily
console yourself."

" So you suppose," answered my lord, as
both quitted the fire-place; " but, believe me,
it will *not* be easily."

Mrs. Robert Spender gathered up her shawl
in silence. The Earl's words, even his tone,
were all her vanity demanded ; yet was she
bitterly dissatisfied. A poignant doubt of his
sincerity crossed her mind, perhaps also her
heart; and it was new to her to suspect a
coming separation to be a matter of greater
indifference to an admirer than to herself.

Not another word was said, and they were
slowly leaving the apartment, when—at the
moment Mrs. Robert set foot in the hall—the
opposite door of the dining-room was opened
from within, and, in the stranger so lately
arrived, a tall, eminently handsome man,

stood before them. Mrs. Robert Spender met the stranger's regards with a gaze much keener and more inquiring than his own, and it was with an astonishment that almost arrested her steps she observed the surprised expression of his eye as it passed to her companion. The recognition appeared to be mutual. A bow was exchanged between the two men, cold on the part of the stranger, and on that of Lord Featherstone something even more than cold; while a quick glance discovered to Mrs. Robert on the countenance of the Earl a singular expression that, in a slight degree, she had observed there on previous occasions when she had supposed him especially ill-pleased. She was compelled to continue her way upstairs, and to forego, for that night at least, all questions on the subject of the rencontre. Her curiosity, however, had been, and continued, so powerfully aroused, that she paused for a moment in passing her cousin's door, and only the ill-humour entertained by her towards Julia on this evening counteracted a tolerably definite desire to enter. It did counteract it, and she went on to her own room.

More than once while making her preparations for retiring to rest, and as rather a welcome diversion of her thoughts from the mortifications of the day, she reverted to the stranger, in whom her quick eye had discovered a man handsomer than the Earl, and at least equally distinguished-looking. " What," she asked herself for a second, and even third time, " could make him bow so gravely to Lord Featherstone? What could make Lord Featherstone bow so haughtily to him? Who can he be? and what brings him here? and is he going to remain ? Just as we are leaving too—how inestimably provoking !"

CHAPTER XI.

A BOSQUET.

> " Grosvenor Square,
> " London.

" The post-mark of this will surprise you. We arrived here the night before last—Lady Featherstone and myself.

" Do you believe you could make it possible to come to us? We propose betaking ourselves to Weymouth, Brighton, Dover—some place that promises gaiety and sea-air ; and are most desirous to include you in our party.

" By Heaven, Fred! I cannot preserve this
tone.   The concentrated, unimaginable bitterness on which I have carried a superstructure
of *nonchalance* boils within me when I sit
down to address you.   My foible is not, I
believe, a too great communicativeness and
unreserve, and my discoveries of the last few
days have not been a sort of which a man is
commonly desirous to prattle; neither am I
ordinarily a person to ask or endure sympathy,
or to own myself a fit subject for it.   Yet, I
declare it to my God—the first, the only relief
I have experienced since I became aware of
the disappointment prepared for me, is at this
moment, when I tell you that than myself,
there does not exist a more vitally wounded
wretch on the face of the wide earth.

" Yea, and I say this even in the hour of
the fruition of a long-coveted revenge.

" It is rare—very rare—with me to find a
laggard to obey me in my pen.   Commonly,
it keeps pace with my imagination, and my
thoughts are scarcely framed ere they are

before me, written words upon my paper. And now I can hardly write a line. It is because I am accustomed to write with levity, and now—*now*—my excitement is real.

"I have regained my self-command. In proportion as I grow calm, however, my sense of injury becomes more blighting; for in this instance, at least, injury is sustained, not inflicted by me. Fred, before Heaven I declare (whatever the unsubstantial fancies of an hour may have induced me to write), that I had no other intention in returning to this country than to do the most absolute and ample justice to the lady who had been so long secretly my wife. I say not what share the manifest insecurity and real illegality of any other similar connexion contracted during her lifetime had in the formation of my resolve. That matters not. From the moment in which the resolve *was* formed, I surrendered myself to the contemplation of the happiness I had every right to expect in such a reunion. I called to mind the affection of which I had

been the object in former years.   I had never
ceased to feel tenderness for the person who
had testified it, and an esteem very different
from the best opinion I had ever entertained
of any other of her sex.   I felt, of course, that
she had been seriously wronged by me.   As,
however, her character had never suffered, as
she probably accused herself of some imprudence of which she would recognise the reasonable punishment in the sorrow it had
entailed on her, and as she had no pretensions
of her own to anything resembling the position that had become mine, I supposed I was
bringing her home a very fair recompense for
all I had caused her to endure.   Solemnly, as
on my death-bed, I believed her incapable of
forgetting me, or dishonouring my memory;
of conceiving resentment, or of even recalling
past grief, otherwise than to enhance the
gladness of the present.

"I returned to England, as you know.   As
you know, too, I lost not an hour in satisfy-
ing myself of Lady Featherstone's existence

and place of abode. You are likewise aware that—indulging a romance hitherto not very prominent in my character—I delayed only long enough to go to some pains and expense in rendering the house I now write from, what it is, and then followed my wife into Radnorshire. As a mere precaution against too sudden and startling a recognition of me in public, I adopted the slight disguise which an unlucky caprice induced me to continue. The little mortification, not unnatural on finding myself regarded as a stranger by a person with whom I had anticipated so different a meeting, overcome, I conceived the idea, in company with other more frivolous fancies of the moment, of becoming the lover of my wife for the second time, and in the character of a new acquaintance. On cold encouragement enough—indeed, by the time I spoke, I believe curiosity, and perhaps a desire to see how far she was to be influenced by the prospect of fortune and a coronet, were my strongest motives—on cold encouragement enough I laid myself open to mortification by a proposal which she decidedly rejected.   The position of an unsuccessful suitor was a new one to me, and you may believe I was not highly gratified.   A man, however, is unwilling to perceive an ill compliment in what is at all capable of a contrary interpretation.   'I communed with my heart, and in my chamber,' and believing I held the clue to such rejection, was presently ass enough to feel even flattered at what assumed the aspect of a faithfulness to me rising superior to sufficiently glittering temptations of wealth and rank.   By the Lord! I shall hardly err on the side of too great a benevolence of opinion again.

" I get on slowly with my narrative, yet it is not so agreeable that I should willingly linger over it.   I have not often had occasion to record myself the dupe of the sex, or of my own too favourable consideration of human nature, and you must excuse the awkwardness

with which I treat the subject, in. consideration of its unfrequency.

" And now, Fred, what think you?   This
lady—this wife, whose grievous ghost had
ofttimes risen amid revels to reproach with
cruelty a certain friend of yours ; this widow,
as she deemed herself, whose injuries I had
come some thousands of miles to repair; this
victim, as I deemed her, of an earthly love,
whose melancholy tears had wept the bloom
from her cheeks, and the light from her eyes ;
whose calmness I attributed to exhaustion;
whose smiles to a religious hope; whose rejection of rank, social position and companion-
ship seemed to me the high-souled indifference to worldly advantages of one cherish-
ing a pious devotedness to the dead.—By
heaven ! I scarcely know what I write—rank
nonsense, I believe; yet, would I not for a
dukedom that any save yourself should guess
how largely bitterness is an ingredient in the
measure of my irony.

"In my last letter from that accursed place which is worse than fever or a sore to think of, I named in a postscript—I think I named in a postscript—the arrival at the boarding-house of Colonel Montresor—Montresor AGAIN. The fiend give me patience to tell you that his errand in arriving there was to marry my wife!

"There was the solution of the problem—the problem of rejection by a woman of a husband and a Peer. Admire its simplicity, sir, in contrast with those that had presented themselves to my mind. She was in love with another man. Engaged to Colonel Montresor; yes, forsooth—engaged! Eternal curses seize his soul.

"I am again calm, but of such calmness let mine enemy beware! I spare you all description of my astonishment when the truth first appeared. Nevertheless, the absurdity of the affair was overpowering. Can you conceive anything more ridiculous than the maidenly modest encouragement of a lover, who, for fastidious propriety of demeanour, might be Sir Charles Grandison himself, by one's own wife, married a little upwards of eleven years ago ? By the gods ! the first vent I permitted my marital sense of wrong was a hearty fit of laughter.

"' Adversity,' the poet hath it, ' wears still a precious jewel in its head.' Now, the jewel in the head of my adversity is, as you no doubt perceive, the perfectness of the revenge that it affords me on the officious fool who has crossed my every path through life ; that is, if he be not—as I fear he may —too cold-blooded a beast to feel as I would have him. From boyhood I have hated him. There is that in his eye—his voice—his very step—that has ever galled me, as no other thing has had the power to do. And I will hate him yet—even yet—more sufficiently to the purpose. This encounter has not satisfied me ; I have been pricked in it myself. My weapon had a double edge, and cut the hand that wielded it. *She loves him.* True, he has desired her, and she is mine, and I stand between her and him.   But, he has rendered her worse than valueless to me.   Be it so — *Il viendra.*

" By the Lord, sir! to see the commotion there was in the place.   The tattlings, the whisperings, the gigglings, the when's, the how's, the why's, the where's;   then the fawning on the bride-elect by her own party, and on her party again by all the others; the upliftment of mine hostess of the Heath House; the beaming satisfaction of Mrs. Robert Spender; with the *comme il faut* demeanour of the engaged pair themselves, the simperings and smilings of the one, the attitudes and attentions of the other; all assisted to compose a broad farce, the like of which has, I should imagine, rarely been seen on any stage.

" I stood aloof, and quietly looked on, for I desired to have perfectly the command of myself before I stepped from my spectatorship on the boards.   And now, before proceeding further, do you desire to hear in what manner the Fates or Furies brought about an acquaintance between two persons who might have been supposed the last two likely to meet? Have I hitherto mentioned Lady W——? Her dowager residence is in the immediate neighbourhood of Westbridge. She was the thorn in the flesh of the mistress of the Heath House—the crook in her lot—the one bitter drop in the otherwise sufficiently fruity cup of her life's enjoyment. Lady W. would not visit Mrs. Fleming. The latter lady had made such advances in the direction of the former as a Mrs. Fleming could make to a Lady W., but in vain. Lady W. would not visit Mrs. Fleming, would not know Mrs. Fleming, would not know of Mrs. Fleming. Neither would she accord her notice to the two young ladies who were so frequently the visitors of Mrs. Fleming, and seen at public places under her wing. It appeared, however, that Julia had not been absolutely unobserved, for, encountering her after her illness and the subsequent marriage of Mrs. Robert Spender, her ladyship was so much shocked (Mrs. F.'s version) by the alteration in her appearance, and so much interested by her look of delicacy and suffering, that she obtained an introduction, called, asked her to West Court, and became so warmly her friend as to draw upon her the neither very just or very generous resentment of her former *chaperone*. A certain December brought Lord W. to the Court. A certain February took him away again, and — the neighbourhood believed—took him away the rejected suitor of the lady who supposed herself my widow. This rejection, however, if it really had taken place, served only to increase the value of the dowager for her *protegée*. In other Decembers Lord W. made others visits to West Court in the position of a consoled and married man; and years went on.

" These brought about the marriage, in its turn, of the second son of Lady W. to a young French woman of noble family, and who possessed an estate in the south.   A visit from the young persons to ——shire followed in due course, and it was with them, on their return to the Continent, that Lady Featherstone made her first acquaintance with Paris last spring.   It was at Paris that she and Colonel Montresor met.

"A month of Parisian gaiety had been all, in the first, intended.   At the close of this, however, entertainers and entertained found themselves so well pleased with each other, that the latter was prevailed on to accompany the former to their estate; and, lo! 'grim-visaged war hath smoothed his wrinkled front,' and turns Troubadour in the chambers of the soft Provençal dames.

"For me—I was at this time gazing at an imaginary coronet in the one looking-glass of my bungalow, while my servant packed my socks and shirts, three pairs of boots, and an armful of eastern trumpery; and for the uncle of the countess *inconnue*, the misanthrope of the square house outside the Westbridge gate

—a letter was on its way from his death-bed and the hastily-summoned and unsupported Diana, to the Mediterranean shores.

" Have I said enough ?   My pen delighteth not in the episode, and is broken by the force with which it has just met the bottom of the ink-bottle.   I take a new one from my desk, and return to Wales.

" I have said I stood aloof and looked on. I suffered four and twenty hours to elapse, and only on the afternoon of the day succeeding that in which the engagement of the supposed Miss Verity to Colonel Montresor had been permitted to transpire, did I sit down to address myself to the betrothed of that officer. It was not a long letter that I wrote.   Indeed it was quite otherwise.   Nevertheless, it acquainted her with my existence; and without discovering my identity, it informed her that I awaited a personal interview with her in a certain arbour somewhat removed from the public eye ; and it bore the signature of ' Philip Vaughan.'   It was, at the proper time, deposited on her ladyship's dressing-table, where she could not fail to find it on retiring to her room, at the conclusion of the third meal of the day, to reflect for a few minutes on her felicity, and retouch her toilette for the remainder of the evening.

" It was nearly dark when I entered the bosquet ; and as the night, though not rainy, was cold, louring, and autumnal, a *tête-à-tête* was the less likely to be interrupted. I waited alone a considerable time, and long after I conceived she must have found and read, and re-read my letter, I could discover no indication of her approach.   I even began to suggest to myself the possibility that she might be induced by the extremity of her position to deny some passages in her former life ; and commenced to examine whether, favoured by the circumstances that had surrounded our union, there existed the barest chance that she might do so with success.   These speculations were, however, put to flight by her advancing footsteps on the gravel.

" Beneath the trees I was enveloped in a profound darkness, but the light of a moon beginning to be visible, was on her face. I could not resist giving my revenge the satisfaction of contemplating her advance from between the leaves. I had the compliment of discovering that her eyes were full of anguish; a deadly pallor had possession of her features; her limbs seemed scarcely capable of sustaining her; and, in short, she presented so much the spectacle of a person utterly overwhelmed that—but it was not at such a moment that I could regard her with pity.

" When she entered the shadow of the trees that hid me from her sight, she paused. It seemed that her strength could support her no further; and the moment was now come in which it was necessary for me to intimate my presence. She could have very imperfectly discerned the figure that approached her, that addressed her by her name, that led her into the *bosquet*, and seated her by his side. I spare you the raptures I considered proper to the occasion, and to which she responded only with tears. I believe, on retrospection, the concealed bitterness of the previous four and twenty hours must have rendered me more cruel than I would have been in cooler blood. I had suffered too much myself not to have a sufficiently malicious enjoyment of her sufferings, which were in themselves calculated to provoke a still greater vindictiveness of resentment. Every second word of mine must have wrung her heart. I had not failed to perceive that penitence on my part was unneeded. So self-convicted did she stand, and conscious of the wrong I had sustained in her affections, that she beheld in me the most injured of men. It was not till I had said everything I considered likely to be most torturing to her feelings, and concluded such history of the last eleven years as I thought fit to relate, that I began to affect astonishment at her silence.

"'It is, indeed,' I said, 'long that we have been separated ; but what are years or tens of

years to the love we pledged to each other for
eternity ?   Every former recollection forbids
me to suppose that this reunion is affording
less happiness to you than to myself.   How !'
I exclaimed, ' do you not hasten to give me
assurance of this ?—What am I to believe ?'

" ' Alas !' she answered in a voice the
most heart-broken and utterly pathetic that
can be conceived, ' believe that I shall desire
your happiness beyond my own.'

" ' What language,' rejoined I, ' is this ?
Desire *my* happiness !   Are these the words
of Julia ? '

" I felt that she was weeping.

" ' Have I,' I exclaimed, with indignant surprise, ' set phrases—smooth sentences of po-
liteness to listen to ?   It is, perhaps, that you
are uncertain of my worldly position,—that
you believe me a broken adventurer returned
to disgrace you in the eyes of your gayer and
wealthier friends, and compel you with the
authority of a husband to participate in his
ruined fortunes ? '

" ' No—no! believe me, no!' she replied with much feeling and unmistakable sincerity. ' *Disgrace* ' and ' *adventurer* ' are impossible! And if you have not had success—if you are not in prosperity—my duty is the more distinct.'

" I hastened to deprive her of the pleasure of generosity—of the consolation of self-sacrifice.

" ' My success,' I said, ' has been beyond my hopes. My position is probably beyond your imaginings. Your friends will not have cause to pity you. We shall instantly quit this place, however; and, since so many years have elapsed since we last met, and you are much changed, for I have already seen *you* when you least suspected it—have you no curiosity to behold the person—as he now is —with whom you have to pass your future life ? '

" I felt her shrink from me as I spoke; and feeling it did not incline me to spare her. Something she said of having forgotten there would be any change.

"'Yet you,' I rejoined, 'are altered.'

"'Illness,' she said, 'has altered me.'

"'And I, too, may have been ill. In fact, I have been so. Though alive when you believed me dead, I possess no charmed life, and years and suffering have done their work. Come and see.'

"She rose,—obeying me almost immediately. Yet there was reluctance in the movement, too.

"'Come and see.'

"The moon struggled with heavy clouds, but was then shining; and I led her—not the moon but the lady—to the entrance of the bosquet, clear of the trees. Then I turned my face towards her.

"Not at once did she recognise me. It was gradually that perception took possession of her features, and as it did so their ghastliness became extreme. The hour, the moonlight, may have heightened this. However, when the perception I have spoken of—the conviction—became complete, she fell, without a word, without a sound even, to the earth.

" I forbear to describe my feelings in contemplating her. Thank God, they were short-lived! But if ever I could have been a Cain it was in those moments.

" I forbear, indeed, to dwell further on any part of the scene. Its bitterness has subsided having filled, however, a cavity in my heart, which—like a certain deep pool in the grounds at Carysbrook whose margin afforded but treacherous footing—is unsafe to approach, and marked ' dangerous !' by me.

" To proceed, Lady Featherstone once restored to consciousness— to comprehension,— a very few minutes were sufficient to possess her of my meaning. I gave her one hour to make such preparations as were indispensable to her journey; I prohibited the exchange of a word with Colonel Montresor or any other person than her cousin; and I enjoined her to acquaint this last, with a view to the subsequent and decorous enlightenment of the public mind—with the revelations of the evening. The good sense and good taste of Mrs. Spender did not, I take leave to conclude, on this occasion desert her. No alarm, or even uneasiness was created, and at the expiration of the time named, a chariot containing Lady Featherstone and myself rolled from the door, to the unmitigated astonishment of the only two persons who witnessed our departure, and to whom, as I drew up the glasses, I profoundly bowed.

"We passed the night at B——, for I considered it undesirable to superadd bodily fatigue to the mental distress that Lady Featherstone had undergone; but at an early hour the next morning we were again on the road, and with four horses and as few delays as might be, made our journey to town. I am happy to say she bore it well, and that, on the whole, her health has suffered less than might have been expected. Yet she looks ghastly.

" Now, in the relation I have given you of my interview with Lady Featherstone, you cannot have failed to be struck with one thing,—she never inquired after her child. She has done so since. As the grave had given up the one fraction of humanity she had supposed within it, it was but to be expected that she would question the veracity of the statement that had reached her as to the entombment of the other; and had she questioned in the first instance, I should probably have suffered her to know the truth. Further consideration and more recent intelligence that I have received have convinced me of the inexpediency of permitting her to become aware that her child exists. I know not that it does exist! Need I tell you I had not been forty-eight hours in England before an agent of mine found himself at —— ? The girl— woman I should say—and the family of the woman, had quitted the place. In this there was, at first sight, nothing extraordinary; nor, occupied as I was with still more important anxieties, did it occasion me any alarm. Investigation, however, has convinced those who have made it, that the woman has not only quitted ——, but quitted it designedly without leaving any clue by which she might be traced. No child was ever seen with her while she remained at ——, and she left after changes in her family that rendered her leaving a very natural step. She is believed by persons in the neighbourhood of her former residence, and by those she formerly knew, to be still unmarried, but of this belief no reasonable explanation whatever could be given; and a rumour that she is now travelling on the continent, either as companion or lady's-maid in an English family, proved on enquiry at least equally vague and unaccountable. My confidence in her remains unshaken, and after much thought I have come to the conclusion that the child never lived to need her personal care. Had it done so, she would not have put it thus out of my power to communicate with her respecting it.

As for the money—and it was a very trifling sum, though important at the time to me—it was to be hers absolutely, in any case. Moreover, if she has kept an eye, which is at least probable, on my fortunes, she would feel that to offer back any part of that paltry sum would too much resemble the putting in a claim for more adequate remuneration.

" I have bestowed much thought, and some feeling on the matter; and in convincing myself that the child is dead, convince myself also that, under the circumstances, it is well dead.   It must be my endeavour to atone for my abandonment of it by the greater care of those to be born to me.

" And now I conclude my letter as I began it with an urgent entreaty to you to come to me if you can.   There is not in England the man save yourself whose society I could desire at the present time; yet I feel that to prolong the matrimonial duet will probably be destructive of all future harmony.   The looks and voice and manner of Lady Featherstone grow daily colder, and Time, which is recovering her from the shock her violent change of prospects caused her to sustain, only increases the distance between her and myself. This is but natural, since as her mind regains its strength, her appreciation of my past conduct and present motives becomes clearer. My wish is to protect her as much as possible from dwelling upon these. You will easily believe that in making a reunion with my wife I could have no intention of leaving myself without an heir, nor can I desire to live on terms of positive disinclination with the mother of my children. Though I had hoped very different things from what are, or can now be, in a reunion with the bride of my youth, she shall find me, if not otherwise by her own fault, at least a polite and attentive husband. She is eminently ladylike, the world will call her beautiful; she will be admired in society, and may—provided she have the sense to accept it—enjoy, I should imagine, a very fair share

of happiness. I desire you distinctly to understand that if I have named such a word
as 'jealousy'—and I know not that I have—
it is jealousy of the purest affection of her
heart that I meant to indicate. I have the
most entire and unlimited confidence in her
principles and honour.

"Colonel Montresor is in town also. I
passed him in Rotten Row this morning.
With him was a little girl whose flaxen hair
streamed over her riding-habit; the child, I
imagine, of Lady Susan Corfe. My child
would have been nearly the same age.

"I shall anxiously expect your reply, and
shall be ready for departure in the hour it or
you arrive.

"Yours faithfully,

"FEATHERSTONE."

CHAPTER XII.

CONTAINS TWO SHORT LETTERS.

[Letter 1.]

" My very dear Lady Featherstone,—

" I have been hoping to hear from you. Many considerations have withheld me from an earlier intrusion ; but it is now more than two months since I have received a line, and I am an impetuous woman and cannot endure to be silent any longer.   Moreover, I am an *old* woman and cannot afford to be silent any longer.   If our former intercourse must cease, let a new one begin this very day.   With my newspaper in my hand, I am not ignorant of where you are.   But I want to know more than this.   I want to know how you are.   I want to know what you are doing and what you are going to do; and to beg you to make my compliments acceptable to your lord; and to sign myself again, my dear Lady Feather-stone,

" Yours most affectionately,

" SOPHIA W."

" West Court,
   " Westbridge,
     " November 24th.

————

[Letter 2.]

" MY DEAREST LADY W.,—

" I thank you very much for your kindest of letters, and gratefully accept your permission that a new intercourse shall commence from its date. For *one* minute only, and for *once*, I will go further back. I think it due to your long and great kindness to tell you that Colonel Montresor knew all of my history that I knew myself.   He knew that I had been a wife—had been a mother.   I tell you this to vindicate myself, and yourself, in your eyes; but I have yet another motive. Dear Lady W.! from the fact that his regard outlived such revelations as I have mentioned, you will draw the inference that I draw,— that he needs at this moment all the sympathy, all the tenderness of those he values. He will not *seem* to suffer, and it is because he will not that I have written to you what I would not have written to any other person in the world.

" We leave this place in two or three days for Cheltenham. We have made a short visit to Tudor Hall, but found it in a state not habitable, and to make it so would require a larger sum of money than Lord Featherstone is disposed to spend on it just now. We shall remain, therefore, I believe, at Cheltenham, till Parliament meets.

"God bless you, dear Lady W.! Say more of yourself, I beg of you, in a second letter. I am already better since I have received your first. Pray for me, dear friend; and oh! above all things pray that I may come to pray more and more faithfully for myself.

"Forgive me,—I should sooner have thanked you. I will present the compliments you kindly send to my lord on his return—he went to London this morning—and am, dearest Lady W.,

"Yours ever affectionately,

"JULIA FEATHERSTONE."

"Brighton,
  "November 26th."

END OF BOOK I.

BOOK II

NETTINE.

CHAPTER I.

A MOTHER AND DAUGHTER.

" AND when, then, does she come ?"

" As soon, I suppose, as we can receive her."

The above sentences were spoken by two ladies, of whom one was young, the other what is, by courtesy, called middle-aged. These are not, however, very definite terms ; and as the sentences recorded were not immediately followed by others, we may employ the next few moments in looking about a little for ourselves.

The first speaker, then, might have been nineteen, and though her likeness to the older, larger, and "fortier" lady left no doubt of the relationship between them, she was exceedingly beautiful. Her features were regular and delicate, her complexion brilliant and blonde, her eyes deliciously blue, and her hair light and abundant. She had probably passed the evening abroad, for a bonnet and shawl lay negligently at the foot of the sofa on which she herself reclined, and her dress had more of freshness and elegance than accorded with that of the older lady or the aspect of the room. The lamp, indeed, that lighted her glittering bracelets and rings, her little black velvet jacket, and her white muslin skirt, lighted also a sofa and chairs covered with yellowish crimson moreen, a carpet out of which the colours had faded, a table cover no longer new, and walls that could not have been lately painted. An upright piano occupied a recess, and a vase of wax flowers stood under a glass shade on the sideboard; but these could not be held to increase greatly the cheerfulness of the apartment.

I have said there was a short silence. A vexed, fretted look had possession of the large though comely features of the mother, while a thoughtful expression that one could not suppose its habitual one appeared in the beautiful face of the daughter. Indeed, the latter presently seemed to have arranged or dismissed her thoughts, and was the first to resume the conversation.

" What do *you* think of it, mamma ?"

" I am sure I don't know what to think of it !" And the person who spoke sat up and resumed her work which had lain for some minutes neglected on the table before her.

" If," said the younger lady, " she really has this beautiful voice, she will be an attraction, I suppose."

The elder lady said nothing.

" And I have sometimes wished that our house—that we were a larger party."

"I don't know, I'm sure!"

"I wonder—is she good-looking?"

"I hear of nothing," said the elder lady, " but her voice. What signify her looks?"

"Why, you see, if she happened to be *very* good-looking, it might signify a great deal to me."

The elder lady was intent on threading her needle, and held it for the purpose close to the lamp, while the younger one rose from the sofa, approached the fire, stooped a little towards the strip of cloudy looking-glass that surmounted the chimney-piece, and proceeded to call into better arrangement first one group then the other of her bright, fair ringlets.

" But, mamma," she said, while this little matter was in progress, " doesn't it seem to you that this sister of papa's must be a good soul ? "

" *I* don't know ! " the elder lady reiterated.

" But, mamma ! "

The " mamma " was silent.

" Why doesn't papa go to her ? "

" How ever can your papa leave his pupils?
—and she doesn't wish it."

" She must be a brave woman. She must
be a good woman, as well as a brave one, to
do what she has done for this girl—what she
is doing."

" A'n't you going to bed? I shall stay up
till your father comes home from Miss Mackenzie Browne's. Who were at the Collins's?"

" Nobody in particular."

" Not Rolleston?"

" No."

" Not Florian?"

" No."

" A'n't you going to bed?"

" I think I want some supper. I have only
had cakes, and a jelly, and an ice. I should
like some cold meat."

" At this time of night? Your father will
have supped ; and I have had my bit of what
I wanted an hour ago. There *is* no cold
meat."

"Some bread and cheese, then, and some beer."

"Dear me! Well, call to Marianne."

And the young lady did call to Marianne, and requested her to bring the viands she wished for, returning again, however, directly afterwards to the position she had before occupied between the parlour fire and the parlour table.

"I suppose," she said, "Nettine is short for something. It sounds like French. Was the father a Frenchman?"

"Caroline!" ejaculated the elder lady, out of patience at last, "it is not a subject for a girl like you to talk of."

"Pooh!" said Caroline.

"And if—yes, that will do, Marianne— you may fill the glass,—and bring the salt, please—and if the girl is to come here, and I am to associate with her, I may just as well know all about her first as last."

"I don't know all about her myself."

" *Mon Dieu !* Has she such a history ?"

" A history that it is not very pleasant for your father to talk about ; and he don't talk about it more than he can help."

" Perhaps," observed Miss Caroline, " there is no niece in the case. Perhaps she is the poor woman's daughter."

" Perhaps nothing of the kind !" answered the elder lady, and pushed away her work, and leaned back in her chair, as far, that is to say, as the limits of such a chair would permit. " You are very inquisitive," she said, a little angrily, " but of course you must know all about it first or last. Only don't go hinting at what you know to your father—or to the girl herself—"

" I should be more likely," observed the young lady, " to hint at what I don't know."

" Or chattering about it to the Collins's."

" Mamma ! do you think I am a fool ?"

" I don't know that you have much wisdom to spare. However !—your father's father was a professor of music the same as he is—

you needn't ask where, because I am not going to tell you. He was a professor of music, and buried his first wife and married a second when your father was about six or seven years old."

" Oh !" interrupted Caroline, " it is a history with a step-mother."

" Yes ! As yours is a history with a step-father. And I don't think you have much cause to speak against step-mothers and step-fathers, Caroline."

" Certainly not. Go on, mamma."

" I gather from your father that the second wife was quite a young woman, and dressy, and not regular in going to church, or any place of worship ; but a good temper, and kind to him,—always putting in a good word, if one was wanted, with his father, and speaking up for him to their friends. So they all went on together very well as long as the little girls—she had two—were young, and the father living. Just as they, however, began to grow up, he got rheumatic fever, and died,.

and this made a change. Your father had already a good deal of teaching, and the prospect of more in time, and his boarding would, of course, have been a help, so an arrangement was come to amongst them that he should make the step-mother's house his home. For some little time he did so; but he saw things going on that he didn't like. Foolish dress, and acquaintances he didn't approve of, and the girls idling and flirting, and not taking to do anything for themselves, though they had been brought up to be daily governesses. So, finding he couldn't be listened to, and that the mother rather encouraged it all, he made up his mind to leave them; gave over his teaching, packed his pianos and books and what belonged to him, put all straight in the way of money matters, and came off to Bath, where he soon found friends, and married, and began to make the connexion that has become the excellent one it now is.

" And, meanwhile, what he often thought would some day happen, *did* happen; and when it came to this the mother took no blame to herself, but put it all on the poor, foolish girl, and sent her adrift; and for many a day and many a month your good father was her best friend. From a distance, though. He never saw her, and after a while, when the trouble she had brought on herself was a little over, I am afraid she went wrong again. There—it's dreadful to talk about!"

"Go on, mamma."

" Well, she went away to France with someone, and there—and before very long— she made her grave—your father knowing nothing of it—of her death, I mean—at the time. But the other sister—Fanny and Bella they were—the sister Fanny knew; for when, about two years further on, the mother was taken, she (Fanny) crossed the water and brought back the child, and has maintained it ever since ; and her sister's end being a lesson to her, seems to have lived very strictly herself."

" And now *she* is dying ?"

"Now she is dying—or, at least she has some complaint that she is told she can't recover from; and she wants to get her niece settled in a home before she becomes too ill to give her mind to the matter."

" And die by herself, mamma?"

"She writes that she lodges in the house of a woman who is like a sister to her, and that she wants for nothing.   Indeed, since she is able to offer your father the money she does offer with—"

" Nettine—"

" It is quite certain that she does want for nothing."

" Then it will be a regular apprenticeship? —no charity, or anything of that sort?"

" Oh, no ! not as to money—"

" How lucky that she has this voice !"

" Quite a Providence.   In her letter to your father the poor creature—the aunt—says that for some years, indeed till within the last few months, when this voice began to show itself, she was terribly anxious.   Her intention had been to bring up her niece, as she had herself been brought up, to be a governess ; but either through not having the knack to teach, or the girl being slow to learn, she could make nothing of it. It *is* quite a Providence. It is to be hoped, poor soul, she thinks it so."

"The aunt—or the niece ?"

"Both. I was thinking of the aunt; but I suppose the niece is likely to think as the aunt does. Will you ever have finished with that cheese ?"

"I *have* finished with it. Shall I call Marianne ?"

"Marianne !—I should hope Marianne was in bed and asleep before this hour. I shall trouble you to take that dirty plate and glass to the kitchen yourself ; or—if you mind the crickets—you may put them in the corner behind the middle door. The girl will see them when she comes down stairs in the morning."

CHAPTER II.

OTHER ANTECEDENTS.

BEFORE going further, it may be well to say a few words of the antecedents of the second wife of Mr. Arnold, whose name appeared in large letters above " Professor of Music," on a brass plate affixed to the gate of a strip of garden that fronted his house in Upper Camden Place. A little way on a similar gate, without any brass plate at all, admitted visitors into a similar garden, embellishing the residence of " the Collins's," who await an introduction to the reader. But of Mrs. Arnold first.

She was the daughter of a portrait-painter, and of a lady who gave lessons on the piano and in singing, to beginners in a few private families, but chiefly to the younger classes in schools. This lady had seen better days, being the child of a tradesman once in opulent circumstances, but who had become bankrupt, reducing her--the object, poor thing, of a showy but superficial education—to the ill recompensed toil of second, or third-rate general daily tuition, from which extreme necessity, at least, her marriage had relieved her. Mrs. Arnold, *née* Marion Gilbert, was the only child of this widow, and was born in Bath, where her parents resided.

Hearing a considerable jingle of music at home, and being also a good deal in the society of more able professors of that art, who, in common with those of painting, frequented the house of Mrs. Gilbert, the young lady began early to develop powers which her parents were easily persuaded to believe might be turned to profitable account on the stage. They discovered, or were perhaps shown, that she possessed considerable good looks, aptness to learn, and a retentive memory, some humour, some observation, a full average share of self-possession, and withal a tolerable voice. I could easily ascertain in what year she made a very successful *début* on the Bath stage; but the date is immaterial. The popularity of the young lady was considerable, and the importance this gave her in her own private circle aided her attractions in obtaining for her many admirers. None, however, seem to have been very eligible till, at a party at a house where her parents and herself visited, she was introduced to Mr. Datchet.

This gentleman was about fifty years old. He possessed a moderate independence, rented a small house in a quiet suburb of London, was grave, respectable, a widower of some twenty years standing, a scrupulous observer of the ordinances of the sect to which he belonged, and an utter condemner of plays, theatres, and all stage performances whatever. Probably it was for this last reason, and to exhibit the consistency for which human nature is remarkable, that he almost immediately paid his serious addresses to Miss Marion Gilbert.

That the young lady accepted him, surprised and displeased the public. The young lady had, however, this cleverness, to know herself better than the public knew her. Underneath her popular sprightliness, love of her profession, and taste for gay society,— underneath this general carelessness of her exterior, she had long entertained a secret and increasing esteem for things more substantial than a garland of flowers, less evanescent than the applause of the pit and upper boxes. She appreciated the merits of a silk gown over a muslin one, and could imagine that it must be more agreeable to receive attendance, than to wait on herself and others. She had likewise

a large leaning towards such unromantic
comforts of life as good eating and drinking,
with the leisure necessary for the enjoyment
of them. In respect of these last, she perfectly
accorded with her husband ; and being fortu-
nate in beginning together on so good a foun-
dation, they grew without any extraordinary
difficulty to assimilate in other things. The
importance she found conceded to her in the
circle of her husband's friends, flattered her
into complacency towards its dulness : nor
was it till Mr. Datchet's death, when she
found herself the recipient of a merely comfortable annuity that would expire with herself, and (having lost two children) the mother
of a beautiful daughter wholly unprovided
for, that she turned her thoughts to other
scenes. Remembering her own early triumphs,
and beholding the far more unquestionable
loveliness of Caroline, she carried her eyes at
once out of the narrow circle in which for
something like sixteen years they had been
satisfied to remain, and looking boldly to and

across the stage, beheld, opening beyond, a vista, to terminate in the marriage of her daughter to a man of rank or fortune.

It fell out that her own second marriage interposed. In the course of one of Mr. Arnold's holiday visits to London, he was introduced to Mrs. Datchet. Bath recollections and sympathies thus revived, tended to improvement of the acquaintance. Mr. Arnold had not long been a widower, and was childless. The beauty and brilliancy of Caroline cheered him ; the cordial hospitality of Mrs. Datchet was the sort of thing he now began to think he would like to see exercised in his own home. The prospects of the daughter were sufficiently uncertain to interest him in her behalf ; while the present income of the mother would enable him to lay by for the future, out of his own exertions, in a manner he had never yet found it possible to do. His friends were, I think, a little surprised when they were introduced to the second Mrs. Arnold. This surprise, however, was greatest

at the first.   The little ménage went on in a
way that left no fault to be found with it.
Neither mother or daughter were disimproved
by the graver mind of the master of the house,
and all thought of the stage for Caroline was
given up.

Mrs. Collins had greater pretensions to
original gentility.   She was the daughter of
a captain in the army, and the grand-daughter
of a clergyman.   When she was about eleven
years old her father died, and his widow,
being still young, pretty, and by no means in
affluent circumstances, betook herself to a gay
watering place, and to society therein ;—re-
taining her daughter long enough to encourage
a taste for visiting and the compliments of
gentlemen, and then sending her to complete
her education at a third-rate boarding school
in the neighbourhood of London.   From this
the young lady returned at sixteen, as grown-
up, to her mother's house ; and in the midst
of rather ambitious preparations on the part
of Mrs. Linwood for the coming " season,"

thought fit to astonish the public mind by eloping with a young professor of the flute,—the how, the when, and the where of her previous acquaintance with whom, remain a mystery to all but themselves up to this day. Mrs. Linwood was much pitied, and indeed the shock and distress she sustained were extreme. As, however, it presently appeared that she was herself on the eve of an imprudent, though as to family and station not an unequal, marriage, her indignant refusal to regard again as a daughter this rash and ungrateful girl, was, it is to be feared, the less heavily felt.

For this last—she had not, perhaps, married so ill as was supposed; not so ill as she had deserved. The young professor had genius, and a sweet and even temper, and was a gentleman in mind and manners. He had many friends—some far above his own station —who admired and esteemed him; who frequented in a quiet and intimate way his house, flirted mildly with his wife, caressed his little girl, and did not, after his death (which occurred about fourteen years from the date of his marriage), turn their backs on his widow and her daughter. Consulted by Mrs. Collins, they pointed, one and all, to the stage, for Anastasia's career. Some one amongst them, acquainted with a nobleman great in music matters generally, brought the dead flute player to his recollection. His Grace, prompt and benevolent, called the next day on the widow, saw Anastasia, and confirmed the decision of her advisers. Henceforward he was her patron.

Nor did she discredit his sagacity. Of a Bath public (for it was on a Bath stage that she was to fit herself for a more ambitious attempt) she instantly became a favourite. She had not extraordinary beauty, she had not—as a singer—any great science, she had not a marvellous voice; but she had (what some who have voice, science, and beauty, have not) the art to please,—and it was this that the Duke descried in her.

Between two young ladies in the positions of Anastasia and Caroline, and living only four doors from each other, there might be much friendliness, but could hardly fail to be some rivalry. Anastasia was, as far as had yet appeared, the cleverest ; Caroline was the most beautiful. Beyond this, the first had the advantage in some respects, the last in others. Miss Collins might (and no doubt she did) envy Miss Datchet her unprofessional *status* and leisure time; Miss Datchet might (and I have very little doubt about this, either) envy Miss Collins the opportunities afforded her. Indeed it was to these professional opportunities that Caroline owed the most brilliant hours of her present existence. In Mrs. Collins's drawing-room her charming face ceased to " blush unseen ; "—unseen, I should say, by those who would have neither much hesitation or much difficulty in expressing to her their appreciation of its charms. The house of Mr. Arnold, though hospitable, was chiefly so to musical professors of his own

age and standing, and to amateurs more en-
grossed by the music, and especially by their
own share in it, than the professors themselves.
Amongst these were considerable curiosities
—old Mr. Templar, for instance, with his new
wig and his *fade* old compliments, offered
with civil impartiality equally to mother and
daughter—and Caroline might have derived
some amusement from them but for the different style of thing to which the evenings
four doors off were beginning to accustom her
—evenings in which Captain Rolleston and
Co. did *not* compliment Mrs. Collins equally
with the younger female occupants of her
drawing-room.

It was, however, sometimes an annoyance
to Caroline to feel that entirely to Anastasia
she owed the opportunities of listening to
these not unimpartial compliments. It was
mortifying to Caroline to be sometimes made
aware, by the words or manner of Anastasia,
of her consciousness of power in this respect—
Anastasia, whose temper was a little variable

—Anastatia, who could be slightly bitter on the subject of those "grand, but slow" *réunions* in the house of Mr. Arnold, at which the highly esteemed mammas of some of his pupils were accustomed to assemble, and which the Collins's were not invited to attend —Anatasia, who did not always forbear to exercise the "art to please," in successful defiance of Caroline's pink cheeks and brilliant eyes—Anastasia, who had within the last week attracted, and commenced a demonstrative flirtation with, a certain Sir Walter Wing, whose visits, whenever they reached the ears of Mr. Arnold, would have, it was more than probable, the effect of interrupting the intercourse between the two houses. In these circumstances, and assisted by a young person's love of novelty, and a sort of excitement imparted by the very history that was annoying her mother, Miss Datchet found herself able to look forward with some pleasure to the arrival of a companion in her stepfather's niece.

She hoped, indeed, and owned she hoped, that this companion would not prove very good looking. Miss Arnold—no, Mademoiselle Nettine she was to be called—Mademoiselle Nettine was welcome to sing like an angel, if Caroline might only have all the beauty to herself. A little study of the various looking-glasses in the house tolerably reassured her mind on this matter, and the moment of her introduction to Mademoiselle Nettine set it completely at rest. Coming in from her walk one afternoon about a week later than the date of the conversation recorded in the last chapter, a quiet figure seated opposite Mrs. Arnold, on the edge of one of the parlour chairs, rose a little awkwardly at her entrance, and received the thoroughly-good-humoured kiss with which Caroline greeted her.

"Is Nettine," said the latter, "more than just arrived, mamma? I hope you have had a nice journey; and won't you take off your bonnet?"

And Nettine did take it off, and, in taking it off, gave to view nothing more alarming than a small, pale face—of which the only remarkable feature was a pair of large, dark eyes—and an extraordinary quantity of hair, braided smoothly off a forehead too low for the taste of five-and-twenty years since, and coiled once and again, and a third time, at the back of her head in a manner that must have inconveniently filled the not crownless bonnet she had just removed.

CHAPTER III.

IS SHE AN IDIOT?

IT was on a November afternoon that Nettine became an inmate of her uncle's house, and when Caroline and she had quitted the parlour to ascend to the apartment prepared for the latter, Mrs. Arnold drew her chair up to the fender, and began to stir the fire with an energy unusual in the early days of that month when the frost has not yet rendered us quite reckless, and we remind ourselves of the long winter to be provided with coals. Having, then, stirred up this November fire into a very sufficient blaze, she, while remaining seated, while remaining thoughtful, while remaining rather red in the face, exchanged the poker for the hearthbrush, and—still with some liveliness of manner—swept together under the grate the ashes that had within an hour or two fallen from it. Then she rose, and opening a little way the parlour door, waited in expectation.

For her husband, perhaps? No, it was a little earlier than he might be looked for, and she was listening for sounds from a direction contrary to that of the front door. These at length made themselves heard. The girls were descending the attic stairs to the drawing-room, and as they were entering this last, Mrs. Arnold called for her daughter.

Exceedingly bright in the ray of the hall lamp, which Mr. Arnold liked to find lighted, looked the face of Caroline, as she ran down.

" You mean us, mamma," she said, quite animatedly and aloud, " to sit in the drawing-room till tea?" And Mrs. Arnold replied in a similar key and manner that she did mean it, but at the same time beckoned the young lady into the parlour, and almost in the act of closing the door, asked—

"Caroline, is this Nettine an idiot?"

"Oh, no!" replied Caroline, "I think not."

"But my dear, I never saw such a girl! For full twenty minutes before you came in, I could get nothing out of her. 'Yes,' and 'No,' and pulling at her gloves, and staring in my face with those great unfurnished eyes of hers—"

"Oh, mamma, she has magnificent eyes—and such wonderful hair—such a quantity!"

"But do you mean to say that she's like any other girl? I believe she's an idiot."

"Oh, no. I dare say she mayn't be very clever; but, aunt, you know, said she could not teach her to be a governess. And, perhaps, she is not used to strangers."

"Strangers! but, good gracious! Well, we shall hear what your papa says. If she

were six years old—but at sixteen!   Has she
spoken at all?"

"Oh, yes, a little."

Later, when Mr. Arnold was interrogated,
he had not much to say on the subject.   He
was accustomed to the silence of school girls,
and to the quiet manners of older pupils with
their singing masters, and Nettine's silence
and quietness had not, it appeared, struck
him as extraordinary.   He was not disappointed in her voice.   It was a very pro-
mising one.   More he could not say till there
had been practice.

"Your papa," Mrs. Arnold remarked, in the
minute she had alone with her daughter,
when she took leave of her for the night,
"thinks only of the voice; but I don't believe
she's all there.   I never saw such a girl!"

And when Nettine had been a fortnight in
Upper Camden Place, Mrs. Arnold still said,
"I never saw such a girl,"—from a different
cause, however.

In the morning after her arrival, she

(Nettine) had placed herself at the breakfast
table, with eyes not less lustrous than they
had appeared on the preceding day, nor fixed
less frequently or less vividly on the faces of
her entertainers, but having in them a look
of inquiry that, at any rate, did not leave
them absolutely "unfurnished."   The answer
their inquiry received, began, after a while, to
result in her greater ease and more assured
demeanour, in a cheerfulness of countenance,
that the latter had, at first, almost painfully
wanted, and in a gradually increasing interest
in the movements and conversation going on
around her.   Notwithstanding this, she herself remained silent for days, not speaking
even to Caroline, unless spoken to ; so that
when, on occasion of some act or speech on
the part of Mrs. Arnold—something quite
trifling, but that must have seemed comical
to Nettine—she gave utterance to a sudden
merry laugh that vibrated like silver through
the rooms, you may imagine the surprise with
which it was heard.

An inadvertent betrayal of this surprise threw Nettine back, so to speak, for some days. Her new-born gaiety, however, possessed a constitution that enabled it to get over the relapse. In a week the light silvery laugh was once more heard, and after that again and again, and sometimes in moments when it seemed least called for, or was least expected. And this restored laugh began to be accompanied with new manifestations. In her practising hours (and these filled nearly the whole of the short day, for Mr. Arnold, wearied with teaching, would, except when they had visitors, endure no evening music but his own) in her practising hours Nettine was grave, diligent, conscientiously laborious, —for so young a creature, extraordinarily so; it seemed not as if the possibility of being otherwise could enter her mind. But in the moment these practising hours ended, in the smallest interval between them, a necessity for other movement would appear immediate.

November as it was, she would dart, boun--

netless, and in her thin shoes, through the window of the room in which her studies were carried on, and fly round and round the small garden, and back again, and across the plot of grass, in the manner of a young animal set loose from its kennel or its cage, and with a rapidity that would displace the pins sustaining her remarkable *chevelure*, and give it streaming to the wind. This in the first; and when this was forbidden—from no harshness, but on account of the danger to her voice from such irregular exposure—a sort of equivalent was enacted in the parlour. She would laugh, she would sing — not snatches of any exercise or song she had been studying, but strange, spontaneous cadences of surpassing sweetness. She would float about the room, not in a waltz exactly, for she had never been taught dancing, but with some improvised step of her own, that nevertheless carried her round in a manner that was charming to witness. So that, when at the end of two or three weeks, Mrs. Arnold again expressed an opinion that she was " not right in her head," Caroline was quite ready to take her part.

" Do you know, mamma," said that young lady, " I think she has been oddly brought up."

" Probably she has. But many girls have been oddly brought up."

" But I mean *very* oddly. I believe the aunt must be a singular person. I don't gather that they have any friends or acquaintances : and do you know Nettine has never seen fields or trees till she was coming here in the train."

" Many people living in London hardly ever get a peep of the country."

" Ah! hardly ever—But *never* is different! When I happened to say something about the view being much prettier when the trees were green in summer, she looked at me just as I should look at any one who talked to me of astronomy, or anything I don't understand. And then she knows just as little of London,

I did get from her that she never went out except in a little court behind the house, or round two or three streets with her aunt, or to a few shops, near at hand, with the woman of the lodgings."

" You seem to have been very inquisitive, Caroline."

" Well, mamma !—one likes to know."

" I have no doubt," Mrs. Arnold said, " they have lived in a very retired way, which might perhaps explain her being quiet and shy ; but it makes her madcap ways of going on more extraordinary than ever."

" Oh, do you think so ?—I am not sure,— not if it had been her *nature* to be very merry.   She gives me the idea of a butterfly just come out of its chrysalis, only at the wrong time of year.   If it were summer, I should rather expect to see her open a pair of wings, and flutter off over the garden wall."

" Garden wall, indeed !"

There were one or two other matters on

which Mrs. Arnold expressed to her daughter dissatisfaction with Nettine.

"She doesn't seem to me," said the good lady, "to have common feeling. There's this poor creature has fed her and clothed her all these years, and now finds the money that provides her a comfortable home, and though she hears how she is suffering, she doesn't behave as if she had common affection for her."

"Perhaps, mamma, she hasn't common affection for her. You should have seen how she flew about the house for warm water and rag and sticking plaister the day *you* cut your finger."

"Humph! Well—common decency then—"

"And perhaps, mamma, she has never been taught to have 'common deceny.'"

"I never saw your equal, Caroline. You'd argue about the bit of pudding on your plate."

Another grievance—as weeks went by—

was the love of Nettine for finery and trumpery;—Mrs. Arnold used sometimes the one
word, sometimes the other, and in fact they
were synonymous—Nettine's finery being
necessarily trumpery.   A little modest sum
of money was given monthly to Caroline to
spend *properly*.   It was decided in the family
that Nettine should receive a similar sum,
with a similar injunction.   Caroline bought
with hers gloves, and boot-laces, and pocket-
handkerchiefs.   Nettine mended her old gloves,
skipped lace-holes in her boots when the laces
were broken, ignored pocket-handkerchiefs,
and spent her money on trinkets and ribbons.
I do not suppose that Mrs. Arnold could say
she had never seen such a girl in this last
respect, for I think the kind of thing had been
commoner in her own youth than at the time
of which I am writing, and it was commoner
at the time of which I am writing than in the
present day.   Good taste in dress has greatly
progressed amongst the English middle and
lower classes.   But if Mrs. Arnold did not

astonish herself at an eccentricity, she at least
encountered a trial.

And in the meanwhile, though the healthy
nature of Nettine's joyousness was questioned
by Caroline's mother, its self-sufficiency, so to
speak, was abundantly evident to Caroline
herself. Of such plain food, indeed, as comfort, kindness, and a certain amount of permitted independence of speech and action, it
had what was necessary; but of stimulant in
the way of gaiety or expectation, it had nothing. A sum of money had been paid to
the Arnolds to make Nettine a singer, and of
every act of the day this was conscientiously
the object. Not her studies only, but her
food, exercise, hours, indulgences, and res-
traints all tended to this one point. She was
to encounter no unnecessary fatigue, no damp,
no impure air in over-heated rooms. A brisk
walk of half an hour, once or twice a day, on
the pavement in front of the several rows of
houses all known to the uninitiated as Prospect Place, varied occasionally by a visit,

under the protection of Mrs. Arnold, to the
upper air of the Lansdowne Crescent or Rich-
mond Terrace, and, more occasionally still,
and under similar protection, by a descent
into Milsom Street or the nearer Park, formed
her reasonable out-of-door recreation. In-
doors, this last chiefly consisted in laying on
her back, after an exhausting practice, on the
yellowish crimson moreen sofa already mentioned. Caroline thought that to her this
would have been a penance second only in
severity to that of walks taken in the manner
I have related ; and marvelled at Nettine's
happy face; and at her luminous eyes shining
round the parlour, and out on the damp
garden paths, and up to the December sky as
if it had been a sky of June. But then, in
Caroline's case no exhausting practice had
been performed.

CHAPTER IV.

CHARLECOMBE.

By the time, indeed, it came to be December, and while Nettine was taking exercise in the Lansdown Crescent, or experiencing such *dolce far niente* as the crimson moreen sofa and her own untroubled mind could afford, the recreation of Caroline was of a sort that deserves to be recorded.

It was not till the beginning of December that the visits of Sir Walter Wing to the Collins's became known to Mr. Arnold.   He was not a man with any appetite for scandal in general, as may be inferred from the fact that this particular one had not sooner reached him. Nevertheless, when it *did* reach him—this particular scandal—he digested a portion of it, and the result was the interdiction by Mrs. Arnold of her daughter's unchaperoned hours at the house four doors off.

Now, for the loss of Anastasia's society just at the present time Caroline might have consoled herself easily. The young lady who had a baronet for her admirer could, Miss Arnold found, give herself airs; and the mother of such a young lady could permit herself to be inattentive even to the daughter of Mrs. Arnold. But there was an accompanying loss that could not be so well endured. Only at the house of Mrs. Collins had Captain Rolleston and Caroline hitherto met; and I think when the latter pleaded for one more evening—one farewell evening, so to speak—with Anastasia, Mrs. Arnold did not quite suppose that she so pleaded for the purpose of bidding an eternal farewell to the dragoon officer.

Mrs. Arnold found herself at this moment in a position of some difficulty between the distinct duty she owed her husband, and the duty (not quite so distinct) that the recollection of a certain Miss Marion Gilbert inclined her to think she owed her daughter, who was, however, her daughter, and not his. After a really conscientious examination of her perplexity, she came to a compromise between the two duties. The forbidden visits must cease, and beyond these she would, as a wife, be acquainted with nothing that could displease Mr. Arnold, and, as a mother, would interfere with nothing that Caroline—whom she believed she could trust—might deem essential to her prospects. With some skill and still better meaning, and in the opportune matter of Anastasia Collins, she gave her daughter a great deal of good advice, which the reader, if a right-minded person, will hope was not thrown away; and, resigning

herself to the occasion, remained as unconscious as a woman could remain, of several
little elegances of Caroline's out-of-door
toilette that two or three times a week made
themselves seen, and looked down the more
immovably upon her work when that young
lady turned her blue eyes with greater than
usual anxiety towards a threatening sky.

I venture nothing in the way of approval
or otherwise of Mrs. Arnold's line of conduct.
I simply state what that line of conduct was,
and, approve or not approve, could not have
seen without sympathy the brightening of
her still comely countenance, when a furtive
glance had shown her the face of Caroline
radiant on her return from her walk; a
brightening she immediately concealed among
the fender-irons with which it was her wont
to stir the no longer November fire into an
almost undesirable blaze. This radiancy
was, however, not absolutely invariable.
There were occasions when the mother's eye
fell back upon her work, and when her coun-

tenance did not brighten, but became, on the contrary, a little clouded and anxious. I think this anxiety would have been still more observable if she had been quite aware of the extent to which Caroline availed herself of her opportunities. She was aware, it is true, that Caroline's walks occupied a considerable portion of the afternoon. Two people, however, who are pleased to be in each other's company, and have a good deal to talk about, may walk together for a considerable time without getting over much ground; and I am persuaded that Mrs. Arnold, trusting her daughter largely, and not taking into consideration how largely her daughter trusted herself, believed that the young lady and Captain Rollestson were strolling up and down in the field at the end of Prospect Place, or in the road that divided the field from Prospect Place, or in the charming green lane at the back of Prospect Place, at times when they were very remote indeed from Prospect Place, and the field, and the road, and the charming green lane. As far, indeed, as the matter of the mere walk is concerned—its direction and its distance—I see no reason why the reader may not immediately be made wiser than, in all probability, Mrs. Arnold ever became.

On one of those days, then, when Caroline had testified a very early anxiety in regard to the weather, and had been (or might have been) observed pinning a bright, fresh pair of strings into a bonnet faultless in its simplicity, I will invite the reader to pause at about a quarter-past two o'clock somewhere in the vicinity of the gate that had the large brass plate affixed to it. He will perhaps see the unmistakable professor of music come out from it, and take his way, *via* Camden Crescent, in the direction of the town. He will perhaps not see the professor, who may have come out from it and taken the way mentioned, five or ten minutes earlier; but, in either case, he will assuredly soon see a young lady who, having tripped down the gravel path of the garden, will open the same gate daintily, and emerge with a little air half cautious, half indifferent, therefrom. In all probability she will pause for a few seconds after the gate has closed itself behind her. Her eyes will perhaps take the direction that the professor's steps have already taken, and then travel upward to the sky as if a cloud more or less might affect her decision in regard to the disposal of her afternoon. Finally, she will walk away to the left, not at all hurrying herself, but looking here or there at anything that may reasonably attract her attention; and so on till, towards the end of the pavement, where it joins the road already spoken of, a person, perhaps in the undress uniform of a dragoon officer, perhaps in the less conspicuous, but extremely becoming, riding suit of a private gentleman of five-and-twenty years ago, comes into view. Then a bright colour will spring into Caroline's face, and all little affectations vanish in a greeting (on her part at any rate) unquestionably genuine, and grateful, and glad.

Now I am not going to permit eavesdropping to any great extent. When I invited the reader to place himself in the vicinity of the large brass plate, it was that he might become acquainted with the direction and distance of the walks of Miss Datchet *(place aux dames !)* and Captain Rolleston; not with any intention of possessing him of much of their discourse. During a few moments, however, he will not attract notice if he approach the pair a little closely.

They have by this time left the pavement, and having turned round the corner—always to the left—and passed through a gate, are in the charming green lane recognised by Mrs. Arnold as a fit and proper place for such an interview.

"What a dear good creature you are, Carry," said the gentleman, "to walk with me in this way. I was thinking only this morning that if I were not allowed to see you I should cut my throat."

" And I really think," he went on, when a

rather demonstrative pressure by his arm—
for they were walking arm-in-arm—had perhaps, and perhaps not, been responded to by
hers; "I really think it is a change for the
better, these nice country strolls in fresh air,
and only ourselves, from those hot little rooms
and all the rest of it."

Then Caroline felt bound to put in a word
for the hot rooms.   She could do so with
perfect sincerity.   They had been charming
evenings, she ventured to say, and added
almost immediately—

"And then if we had not had the evenings
we should not be having the walks."

This was of course irresistible.   I am sure
the arm must have been demonstrative at
this.

"At any rate," said Captain Rolleston, returning to the subject, " the evenings are quite
the reverse of charming now.   I should not go
near the place only that Wing makes a point
of it, and perhaps it would not quite do to
drop it at once."

" Perhaps not."

" I suppose it will be a match—eh ?"

" Oh ! I am sure I hope so."

" The stage, you see, is the deuce for a fellow who cannot give a title to his wife.   I am glad you are not on the stage, Carry."

" Oh !" Carry said, and at the moment with perfect truth, " I would not have been for anything."

This brought them to the foot of a steep path ascending the cliff,—a path exposed to observation from many points ; and here, as if accustomed to do so, Miss Datchet withdrew her hand from her companion's arm.   I daresay during this ascent their conversation may have been more interesting ; because, you see, while two persons are linked arm-in-arm the attitude is tolerably eloquent, but when they are not so, the little auxiliary of language becomes desirable.   I daresay, therefore, that their conversation was interesting ; but, on the other hand, I almost equally daresay that it was neither original nor unique.   The reader, then, has the less reason to reproach me for keeping him at a distance from it.   At the top of the Cliff they paused—paused, as I think most persons did, and as I suppose most persons, if the path is still there, do—to look round them at a view which, especially on such a brown December day as the one I am writing of, ought to be seen.   They paused, then, at the top of the cliff, and their eyes having gone over the landscape, returned to each other's faces.

" Dear Carry !" said Rolleston, and once more placed her hand within his arm; and the pair turned and walked away towards the fields that are between the top of the cliff and Charlcombe.

The path through these fields, at all times uneven, and on a day like this one a little muddy, kept near to the high hedges, and itself for a considerable part of the way surmounted a bank from whence the pasture made a bold sweep downwards to the valley;

the seclusion of the position being extreme, and the view it commanded always lovely. Caroline was no landscape painter. She did not know that she was a landscape lover. Any taste she might possess for the beautiful in nature had never been cultivated or developed. As she looked and listened, however —(I do not mean listened to her companion, you will understand)—as she looked and listened, she was conscious of an unaccustomed movement within her soul—a movement she had once or twice felt in hearing some fine concerted instrumental music beyond her ability to understand. As for Rolleston, he was guiding her well-made boots and his own, amidst the muddy dangers of the path, and when he did withdraw his eyes from these, found nothing better to say than:—

"What a jolly walk this must be in summer, Carry! We must come here in the summer—the summer evenings."

And then Caroline's heart began to beat quite fast, and there was an end—for that time—of the unaccustomed movement in her soul.

At the end of these fields a gate opened into the lane, or parish road, that, a little lower down, entered the village—this last as small and unpretending and charmingly old-world a one as if it had been situated miles from any large town. Caroline and Rolleston passed through this gate, or rather through the gateway, and turning to the right, went down the lane. They rested a little on the low wall of the old farm, once the Manor house; and Rolleston pelted little stones at a dog that had come out into the green front court to reconnoitre, and seeing nothing worth his notice had lain down just within the outer entrance arch. Rolleston, as he sat on the wall, pelted little stones at this dog, and was moved to observe that if he could write stories he would write one about that house; and, still referring to the summer, remarked how pretty the orchard— planted on a bit of singularly steep and con-

vulsed-looking ground, and weird and unlike
other orchards—must be when the trees were
in bloom. And Caroline said that she thought
a soft winter's day like this seemed somehow
better suited to the scene. And by-and-bye
they were both rested, and got up, and went
on again down the lane towards the church.
I think they never reached the church. I hope
I may not have written a prophetic sentence.
I think they never reached the church. I
think the stile they crossed is arrived at first.
Any way, they crossed a stile, a stile on the
left hand, beyond which they commenced to
ascend—I might say, almost to climb—still
at the side of a hedge, a very steep field
indeed. This last took them a good while,
perhaps because it was so steep, perhaps
because it was the last; for another stile
at the top of it stood also at the top of the
Lansdown Hill, and divided the field from the
Lansdown Road, just where persons taking a
constitutional on that road pause to recover

breath, and give a backward look before they pursue their henceforth level way.

Now, the Lansdown Road is, as all know who know anything of Bath, a very public one; the more so because it is not a road on which there is any traffic in the way of business whatever. It is frequented only by persons, infant and adult, walking or riding for their health or pleasure, and those not in sufficient numbers to offer much shelter to an individual, or two individuals, undesirous of attracting observation. For these reasons probably, Captain Rolleston and Caroline always parted a few yards from the stile I have last mentioned; the young lady getting over it cleverly and unassisted, the gentleman remaining behind for ten minutes' enjoyment of a cigar, or, wanting the cigar, for contemplation of the country, before he followed in her footsteps. But it is Caroline we will accompany.

Terribly am I tempted to touch with my

pen just about half-a-dozen of those five-and-twenty-years-ago personages—*habitués* of that road—for whom certain saucy young folks found *sobriquets*, and imagined histories, and drew caricatures. Terribly am I tempted; but will refrain, the rather because it is my obvious duty to direct the attention of the reader to the wistful glances of Caroline in passing more than one ;party of fashionable-looking persons, in her own shy and hasty descent of the hill. Especially near the corner of the Lansdown Crescent was this wistful glance noticeable. She could not prevent herself from thinking that two or three beautiful young women, included in a group there standing in conversation, might on that very night be partners of Rolleston's in a scene from which she was excluded. Almost his last words to her had been in the following little dialogue :—

" I shall see you, then, on Thursday, Carry ?"

" Oh, yes. I shall be wanting so to know

how you enjoy this ball, and who you dance with."

" Very likely I may not dance at all."

But she looked wistfully at those beautiful young women nevertheless.

Well, you are prepared—or at least it is less my fault than my misfortune if you are not prepared—to feel sorry for Caroline, if she should ever come to need compassion. Yet 1 know not that she can claim much from you in that way. She is not invariably compassionate herself in regard to others. She is hard-hearted in regard to a certain already once-mentioned Edgar Florian, very probably hovering at this moment somewhere about the top of Belvidere, which is, all who know Bath are aware, quite a junction, and can hardly but be crossed from one direction or other by a person residing in Upper Camden Place, on his or her way home. That entrancing tenor is looked at by ladies, greatly Caroline's superior, not at all hardheartedly from the dress or private boxes,

and is known quite in high circles as the
Master of Ravenswood. But this is by gas-
light and candlelight. Miss Datchet has seen
him by daylight, and in the inexorable rays
of the sun, and to the best of my belief
never on the stage at all. So that, to
Miss Datchet he is by no means the
Master of Ravenswood, only "that dismal
Florian," with his black eyes, and his
melodramatic looks, and his eternal blue
satin scarf, and his doubtful gloves. "Gloves!"
I think I hear some critic superbly exclaim,
"What signify 'gloves?' 'The man's the
man for a' that.'" My dear young lady—I
will assume you to be a young lady,—I venture not to lift a male gauntlet—my dear
young lady ! gloves are gloves, and the man
is not always *the* man ; I mean to say he is
not always the man you take him to be. Let
us not aim too high. In the matter of gloves
you need not distrust your own judgment.
I am sure you would not for a moment mis-
stake a half-crown pair for one that had cost

nearly twice the sum. But if you say that you dare equally to trust your judgment in the matter of the wearer of the gloves—why, then I can only shake my head and tell you that you are very rash indeed.

CHAPTER V.

GOING TO SING.

CAROLINE was extremely nice in the matter of her own gloves, and especially of those she wore in her walks with Captain Rolleston. She would often, indeed, take them off carefully in the parlour before she ascended to her perhaps unswept, perhaps swept and undusted, bedroom. I hope I shall not be thought to intend any unkind reflection on the domestic arrangements of Mrs. Arnold. I feel sure that *her* room and that of Mr. Arnold were exactly as they should be from a very early period in the morning.   But with the inferior rooms in such an establishment there are difficulties.   Young ladies have a trick of being a good deal in and out of their own apartments.   They are improving their hair, or admiring their complexions; they are washing their hands, or putting on or off their boots or their bonnets at unexpected hours; and when a general servant—even a conscientious one—has encountered for the fourth or fifth time a bolted door, she arranges with herself to suit her own convenience.

It was, then, a prudent thing of Caroline to remove those well-fitting brown or green or violet gloves in the parlour, and put them smoothly in her pocket, before ascending to her bedroom; and while doing so on the day of which I am writing, she forgot to admire her fluttering ringlets and heightened complexion in the little glass over the chimney-piece, according to her accustomed fashion.   An incident had occurred between the Lansdown

Crescent and Upper Camden Place, of which she shall herself speak to Nettine, who she finds lying on her back in the evening dusk and firelight, with lustrous eyes wandering quite happily over the ceiling. It did not often happen that Caroline found Nettine in the parlour alone.   Mrs. Arnold, I think, put herself designedly in the way of any *tête-à-têtes* between her daughter and her husband's niece.   "Not but what I believe she is very innocent and harmless, and more than half an idiot, poor thing!" soliloquized the good lady; " still, it's all a mystery about her, and—one never knows."   Nettine, then, was not often found by Caroline alone, but on this occasion it happened that she was so (it was rather later than usual, I think), and as Caroline pulled off a glove with a little less than ordinary care, with a little discomposure indeed, the latter commenced the following conversation.

" Where is mamma ?   I have just met the Collins's."

"Oh!—I don't know where Mrs. Arnold is."

"It was so annoying. At the top of Belvidere—as I was coming home—there was Florian,—Mr. Florian, whom you have seen. Well, of course, I could not prevent his walking a little way with me—just to the end of Camden Place" (the handsome building, I must remind you, now known as Camden Crescent was then called Camden Place, which explains the *Upper* on the row of houses in which Mrs. Arnold lived), "and who must we meet but Mrs. Collins and Anastasia, both looking as impertinent and patronising as you please—as if Florian could be anything to me. I felt quite provoked. Are you hearing what I say, Nettine?"

"Oh, yes!—about Mr. Florian, and where your mamma was."

Caroline shrugged her shoulders, and drew off the remaining glove with a rather dangerous impetuosity. Nettine was, however, better than nobody, since Caroline wanted to be talking.

"The inestimable airs Anastasia gives herself! One would suppose she was already Lady Wing; when, on the contrary, people are saying——Mamma declares it is so disreputable that she shall soon cease to visit them, even in the formal way we do. For my part—" But at this moment Mrs. Arnold entered the room.

Now, I think it cannot but occur to the reader that if what he has been permitted to hear of the conversation between Captain Rolleston and Caroline, in the walk that was the subject of the last chapter, were at all a fair specimen of the remainder that he did not hear—and I am in a position to assure him that it was so—I think it must occur to him that the same Captain Rolleston had implied a good deal without very distinctly committing himself to anything. If a lawyer, for instance, should do me the honour to cast his eye over these pages, I am sure he will be of this opinion. A young lady, however, does not look at such things quite as a lawyer does; and I think I am within the mark in saying that nine out of ten young ladies as inexperienced as Miss Datchet, would have found one or two of the sentences that had fallen from the lips of the dragoon officer very agreeable ones on which to reflect. Miss Datchet, at any rate, found them so; and after a little enjoyment of them in her own room, was able to return to the parlour and take her place at the tea-table with a contentment of countenance that sent Mrs. Arnold to her fender-irons immediately.

That lady had, however, all the excuse for mending a good fire that a pretty severe cold could afford. She had been confined for some days to the house; and as, for various reasons more or less distinct, she did not choose Nettine either to walk much alone or to be the companion of Caroline in *her* walks, the child had been, to a great extent, a prisoner.

Neither the little indisposition of Mrs. Arnold, nor the memories of her daughter, prevented those ladies from being observant of a certain air of preoccupation that on this evening distinguished the Professor.   He was never a talkative, never a very lively, man ; but ordinarily when alone with his family, and especially in the evenings when his teaching for the day was done, a quiet cheerfulness characterised him : and whether he spoke more or less himself, he was a pleased observer of, and listener to, all that passed around him.   On this evening he was, however, preoccupied—anxiously, if not unpleasantly preoccupied, his wife and Caroline thought ; and as his eyes travelled more than once in the direction of Nettine, and rested on her—on Nettine, who was the only person unconscious of the fact—mother and daughter exchanged the briefest of intelligent regards.

I know not whether to a second of such regards, or to the unprompted perceptiveness of Caroline herself, was due the *tête-à-tête* in which Mrs. Arnold found herself engaged with her husband almost immediately after the removal of the tea-things. I think we will imitate the discretion of Miss Datchet, and reward ourselves by accompanying her to her attic, in which—having got rid of Nettine—she proceeded to arrange her curls in several becoming fashions, to pull about the contents of a box or two of ribbons and flowers, to draw a little closer her eighteen inches of waistband, and in this way to amuse herself till her ear caught the sounds of the opening and shutting of the parlour door, the quickened, though by no means rapid ascent of Mrs. Arnold to the second floor, and, finally, that lady's unwonted step upon the upper stair.

"Mamma!" Caroline exclaimed when, on rushing out of her room, she found her mother had almost reached it in the dark.

" There—there!" said Mrs. Arnold, " go in! I have something to tell you."

With a momentary reluctance, Caroline followed her visitor. The apartment was not quite in a state to meet unaccustomed eyes.

The trimmings strewed over the dressing-table, the undusted dressing-table itself, the damp towel lying on the seat of the only chair, another festooning the chest of drawers, presented a spectacle only less worthy of admiration than the bed guiltless that day of the housemaid's art. Caroline need not have feared, however. Mrs. Arnold would have sat down *on* the wet towel had not the young lady interposed, when the former immediately transferred herself, and without one objurgatory glance, to the tumbled bed.

" What is it, mamma ?"

" Sit down, child ! Where is Nettine ?"

" In her own room."

" She is going to sing at Miss Mackenzie Browne's."

" Bless me ! When ?"

" When !—on Thursday."

" At the concert—do you mean ?"

Mrs. Arnold nodded, with eyes fixed on her daughter's, and looking unutterable things.

" I *am* surprised !" Caroline ejaculated,

after a little pause. "I thought—Does papa wish it, or how has it come about ?"

"*I* don't know ! No, I don't think he does—much. I suppose he doesn't like to refuse Miss Mackenzie Browne."

"I see. But why in the world couldn't Miss Mackenzie Browne think of it sooner?"

"I suppose because—but, there—your father would be sorry to offend her. As you say, she might have thought of it sooner if she meant to think of it at all.   It is a fortnight ago that she heard Nettine sing, and she must know there is more to do than go to a drawer and take out a gown and satin shoes and all the rest of it. However, we must think what's best to be done."

"Of course. You have not told Nettine yet."

"No."

"And she would not be much use about her dress."

"She ! She'd go like a sweep's girl on the 1st of May. I suppose she must have a satin gown, and a berthe, and you could lend her *your* fan."

"Oh yes!   But do you know, mamma—as you consult me—I really think that so young as Nettine is, and with her beautiful eyes, something very simple would be prettiest.— Just a white net or muslin, with a flower in her hair."

"But with a white net or muslin there must be," said the perplexed matron " a silk or satin slip. So that no cost would be saved, and yet it would not be a silk or satin dress."

"Only so much prettier than one."

"Your father would not think so much of it."

" And besides," continued the young lady, after a thoughtful pause befitting the gravity of the subject, " I don't know that a satin slip would be necessary,—not under muslin. A fine Swiss muslin at the top, with one not quite so fine next it, and a nice white petti-coat under,—and Nettine's petticoats are so very nice, you know."

" It would be so much *making !*" objected Mrs. Arnold, whose rapid mental calculation of the two days' salary of a competent needle-woman, with breakfast, dinner, tea, and supper, and beer at two of the four meals, presented her with no satisfactory result. " It would be so much *making.*"

" I would lend her my silk slip," resumed Caroline, " only it is a little dirty. You know we were thinking it must be dyed."

" Wouldn't there be time for it to be dyed ?" asked the elder lady, catching eagerly at the idea. " It might be dyed blue or pink ; she would wear it the first time as a gown, and it would be a slip for you, Caroline, afterwards."

Caroline shook her head. Dyers were never to be depended on, and a dyed silk not always.

" By the way, shall I be asked, mamma ?"

" I should suppose so," her mother replied. " I shall think it very uncivil of Miss Mackenzie Browne if you are not."

And the countenance of Mrs. Arnold, hitherto expressive only of the cares involved in the matter of the first appearance of Nettine, became more unpleasantly clouded. The trouble, the anxieties, the annoyances she had very dimly, very vaguely foreseen when she first accepted the charge of her husband's niece and pupil, were beginning to have form and colour.

"Of course I should like to go," said Caroline ; "and *my* dress needs only the putting on. However, I think, mamma, if you will give me the muslin for two skirts, and a workwoman—Miss Sewell is the best— for one day, and leave it all to me, I can promise that Nettine shall look very nice."

" And work *your* eyes out of your head."

" Have no fear of that !" replied the girl, and gaily curtseyed to the reflection of those same bright eyes in her little looking-glass, and arranged a ringlet or two at the same time. " You see, papa is so kind."

"That is true!" Mrs. Arnold ejaculated. "And you deserve his kindness, Caroline."

And her comely face glowed up, and I am not sure that tears were far from eyes that had once been almost as beautiful as those of Miss Datchet. She wanted at that moment to ask about Rolleston, but did not ; her wifely heart reproaching her, while her motherly belief in Caroline remained unshaken.

CHAPTER VI.

A CONCERT.

THOUGH rich, whimsical, and, in a small way, imperious, Miss Mackenzie Browne was a gentlewoman.   Of course, therefore, Caroline Datchet was asked, and when the fly stopped at Mr. Arnold's door on the evening of the concert, she descended to the drawing-room, looking so beautiful in a light blue silk dress, and with ringlets surmounted by a double string of Roman pearl, that the Professor paused in his rather anxious walk up and down the apartment, and taking her gloved hands in his, made her two or three of the little compliments he kept especially for Caroline.

" Is your mother ready ?" he then asked.

" I think so. I am but just come down, however."

" And Nettine ?"

" Is in mamma's room. I got her to go and sit there after she was dressed. I thought she might lean back on the sofa and crush her dress, or spoil her hair."

Again the Professor shook his step-daughter's hand with affectionate cordiality, and at the same moment Mrs. Arnold—large, satin-clad, and comely—and Nettine entered the room.

The briefest of glances did Mr. Arnold bestow upon the toilette of the latter, but his eyes rested with more solicitude on her face.

"The child looks very white," he said. " Are you well ?"

" Quite."

"It is her dress, papa,—and the bandoline in her hair," said Caroline, whose critical eye could detect no fault, and who knew that Nettine's whiteness would presently, in a well-lighted room, be more beautiful than the most brilliant complexions of others. She felt for a moment disappointed that Mrs. Arnold did not fully appreciate the result of her labours.

"Mamma!" whispered that young person, touching her mother's shoulders in the cloak-room at Miss Mackenzie Browne's. "Does papa think Nettine is nervous?"

Mrs Arnold had just performed her best smile and curtesy in acknowldgement of the bow of some personage in the apartment, and the pressure of her daughter's gloved finger had nearly made her spill the cup of tea she was at the same instant receiving from a female official.

"I don't know!" she replied, however. "For gracious sake don't put such a thing into any one's head!"

" No. Only I thought he might like to know that she is *not* nervous."

"The less said about it the better!" Mrs. Arnold hurriedly answered, and again her curtesy and her smile were in requisition, " I wish to goodness she had been to sing early in the evening, and have done with it."

Caroline was perfectly right.   Nettine, notwithstanding her youth, notwithstanding what was expected from her, nothwithstanding that she had never been in society—to speak of—before, was not in the least nervous. Indeed, Miss Datchet began almost to have fears of another sort.   Seeing the face of Nettine light up—not with colour, but in the way peculiar to it, at sight of the brilliant staircase, the flowers, the looking glasses, the glittering tea service of silver, and the toilettes of the persons standing like themselves near the fire or grouped around the table, a vision presented itself to her of a pair of gauze wings unfolding themselves from the shoulders of her step-father's niece, and floating the latter,

in the manner of Taglioni or some other Syl-
phide, into the presence of Miss Mackenzie
Browne and her friends.   Happily, the vision
was not realized.   In a very quiet and unre-
markable way, Nettine, conducted by the Professor, ascended the staircase, entered the
august presence, forgot—not through want of
self-possession, but because she was looking
at somebody else—to curtesy to Miss Mackenzie Browne and her friends, and was led
by Mr. Arnold to a chair conveniently near
the piano, and which commanded a good view
of the room, though (and especially when the
ample waist and shoulders of Mrs. Arnold
interposed between her and the company) she
was herself rather out of sight.

It was one of the largest and most brilliant
of Miss Mackenzie Browne's assemblies. The
space left in the centre of the room was
scarcely more than sufficient to permit the
passage of Miss Mackenzie Browne herself,
the performers, and a few other persons, between the piano-forte and the door; while

the smaller room was completely filled with rows of benches facing the business of the evening, in the manner of a pit at a theatre. A single glance around, which had made Mrs. Arnold aware of this, and shown her that the company included the greater number of those competent to judge and influential to pronounce in the Bath musical world, had deprived her of courage to turn her regards on her husband's pupil. For her own sake this cowardice must be regretted, for had she turned her eyes on Nettine—on Nettine, absolutely devoid of fear, anxiety, and self-consciousness—the eyes of the latter, luminous in enjoyment of a scene so brilliant and so new to her, must have relieved the good lady from the greater part of her uneasiness, and might even have afforded her some expectation of a triumph.

As to a triumph, however, it did not arrive. Miss Mackenzie Browne, having carried her point with the Professor, had probably forgotten the very existence of Nettine till reminded of it by the appearance of her name in the " programme" of the evening. Certainly she had not prepared her friends to expect any thing very extraordinary; and as the song that was counteracting the profuse smiles of Mrs. Arnold, and even casting a shade of almost perceptible anxiety over the face of her husband, had not place till just before the conclusion of the first part of the concert, the greater number of the audience had settled to their conversations, flirtations, and so forth, and were not easily to be interrupted by a performance boasting no extraordinary shrieks or *roulades*. A few persons, indeed, of those " competent to judge," rose up here and there from amongst the crowd; the sister and brother artistes were unequivocally, genuinely, and generously delighted ; and even in the inner room, where those least loving music and most given to flirtation were wont to remain satisfied, more than one voice was hushed, when the sweet, clear notes of Nettine made themselves heard. But there was no *furore*—nothing resembling a triumph: only round the piano-forte distinct approval that fully satisfied the Professor.

"Your pupil is charming!" said a little old man from among the audience, but who had been near the piano a great part of the evening. "Her organ is delicious, and your instructions are very recognizable in the purity of her style."

This, and a few such compliments from others, were enough for Mr. Arnold. He had besides ascertained, what it is always so important to know, that Nettine might be depended on; and, though not ordinarily a demonstrative man, he no sooner found himself again in the Fly than he shook hands in the most pleased and cordial manner with the ladies all round.

"I should like to go to such a party every night, mamma!" said Caroline, with the mental reservation, however—"if only Rolleston could have been there!—how provoking of Miss Mackenzie Browne not to invite him!"

It was not till the following morning that Miss Datchet asked Nettine why in the world she had laughed when Mr. Templar was presented to her?

" I don't know," the young girl replied.

" Don't know! but, good gracious —— "

"I think I couldn't help it. He is funny looking, is he not?"

" Yes. But many people are funny-looking in society, and you must not laugh at them."

" And he reminded me of something— and I have seen him often before."

" Mr. Templar!—Where?"

" In Camden Place. When your Mamma has sent me to Brown's or Ball's, I have passed him there. He wears a little white great coat, and a flowered scarf, and perks his head on one side, and I always think his hat will tumble off,—but it never does. And when he is in front of me, I know that he will look up at the windows of one particular house, and I say to myself ' When he comes to *that* stone he will look up.' And he always does."

" I suppose it is his own house."

" I think he lives there.   I have often won-
dered what people live there besides him, and
why they don't come to the windows. But
they never do."

" He lives there alone."

" Such a little man, in that large house !"
observed Nettine, simply.

" And then, who does he remind you of ?"

" Oh! not of ' a who.'   Of a bird on the wall
of our court."

" Our court !"

" Where we used to live. It is not a very
pleasant recollection. It was a back court,
and I had been put out in it one day for a
fault. It was winter, and very cold, and I
was just beginning to cry, when this bird—
not a smooth, fat bird like those in your garden, but an old pinched looking thing—came
hopping quite fast on the top of the wall, and
stopped close to where I was, and twisted his
head on one side, and looked at me so comi-
cally that I burst out laughing. My aunt

heard me and was surprised, and came down to ask me what I was laughing at? and when I said, 'at a bird on the wall,' she was angry and said I had told a fib, and punished me, and I had only dry bread for dinner. So, after all, I had not much need to laugh a second time."

Caroline's face, during the whole of this dialogue had been rather a study. At the conclusion, however, of the above recital by Nettine, she gravely said—

"Papa values Mr. Templar; and he sometimes comes here when we have a little music."

CHAPTER VII.

A DIAMOND CIRCLET.

EVEN Mrs. Arnold had received an impulse to further gaiety at the brilliant concert of Miss Mackenzie Browne, and began to observe that they ought to be asking "a few of their friends." She desired, too, to compensate in some small measure to Caroline, for the disappointment the latter had sustained in declining an invitation to a large party, four doors off, which "an unavoidable engagement" had prevented Sir Walter Wing from attending, but which Captain Rolleston had honoured with his presence. Not that the dragoon officer could, in the present indistinct state of his attentions, be a guest at Mr. Arnold's house ; but it was always a pleasure to Caroline to be wearing an evening toilette, and eating ices, and moving about a well-lighted room. Besides this, Mrs. Arnold was of opinion that since Nettine had sung at Miss Mackenzie Browne's, it was only a proper compliment to " their friends " to invite them to hear her in Upper Camden Place.

A party, then, was given, and was, in its way, and as far as it went, and as it perfectly deserved to be, a success. Mrs. Arnold had not, however, done quite everything that was proper in regard to it, as she discovered on the following evening, and as will immediately appear.

" We might have asked old Templar last night," said Mr. Arnold.

He was walking up and down the parlour in the firelight, just before tea and the lamp were brought in, and his wife looked up with some surprise, as his had been the conclusion that in the present gay month of the Bath " season," it would be—he said unnecessary, but almost implied impertinent—to send an invitation to the petted and flattered and sometimes rather consequential old beau.

" He spoke of it," continued the Professor, " when I met him to-day."

" Good gracious! spoke of it! Was he offended ?"

" Not at all. But he said he would have been delighted to come. He wants to hear my ' Recreations' and Nettine again, and almost invited himself here for to-morrow evening."

" You don't mean that he is coming ?"

" Certainly I mean it."

Mrs. Arnold stirred the fire.

" It need not," her husband continued, as he opened the door to admit the lamp, " put any one out of the way. I shall not ask a soul."

" We shall want to be in the drawing-room, I suppose ?"

" The drawing-room, of course.   And you will give him a cup of coffee, or a glass of lemonade.   That will be all."

It was very fine to say " that will be all," but it was just the sort of "all" that *did* put Mrs. Arnold out of her way extremely. Her little parties—which were, indeed, tolerably large ones—were simple affairs in comparison.   In them she was, in every sense of the phrase, quite at home.   In them she gave, of course, tea and coffee, ices, rout-cakes, and lemonade; but then, Ball, the fruiterer, a most gentlemanly-looking and mannered man, and quite the head waiter at all the finest parties in Bath, took the management of everything, and Mrs. Arnold's mind could hospitably preserve such a serenity as permitted her to do herself justice in the reception of her guests.   To receive a visitor, and a visitor like Mr. Templar, *en famille*, was another matter.   She distrusted herself; she distrusted her general servant ; she distrusted Caroline.   She distrusted everything and everybody except Mr. Arnold, who would be equal to any occasion.

She need not, however, it turned out, have distrusted Caroline. The latter had become pretty well acquainted with the sort of thing at the house four doors off, and could inform her mother that tea, at the hour Mr. Templar proposed to arrive, would be unnecessary, and that, later in the evening, a tray of lemonade, ices, and cakes could with great propriety be placed on a table by Marianne, without any carrying round at all. This important point so satisfactorily disposed of, Mrs. Arnold could, with a relieved mind, prepare her head-dress and her smiles for the occasion.

Occupied with these, she failed to perceive that when the evening arrived, Caroline, notwithstanding her love of toilette, ices, and a lighted drawing-room, was by no means in her usual force or looks. I think had Mrs. Arnold perceived any shortcomings, she would have placed them to the account of her daughter's anxiety for the success of the ar-

rangements she had taken on herself. I am
better informed. *I* know that a rather short,
rather unsatisfactory walk with Rolleston had
concluded at four o'clock that afternoon in
the following manner.

"On Saturday, then, you really leave?"

"On Saturday. Could we have a walk on
Friday?"

"Oh, yes! As far as I am concerned."

"If I *can* manage it I will. I may not be
able, however; and do not expect me beyond
three o'clock. At all events you will see me
again in a fortnight at the furthest. I shall
not extend my stay."

If a little mistrust of the propriety of Nettine's behaviour to her uncle's guest were ad-
ding to the care that appeared in the charming
face of Miss Datchet, that must soon have
vanished. The gravity of the young singer
was undisturbed by the entrance and reception
of Mr. Templar, and even when—having received his compliments to herself—she turned
to Caroline and said "He *is* so like the bird!"

her seriousness of countenance remained immovable.

During the preliminary ten minutes' conversation, and while the Professor played, the two young ladies sate together. So long as that performance lasted, and during a song sang by Nettine herself, not a word was spoken, and Mr. Templar, standing at a little distance from the piano, had not lost a note. When, however, Caroline left her chair to shine forth in "I know a bank" with her mother, and Nettine remained alone, the old amateur—with a smile on his features that could hardly be considered to give him an advantage as to expression of countenance over the feathered animal he recalled to her mind—the old amateur approached her.

He bowed, and with one hand he played with his eye-glass. He always *did* bow, and he always did play with his eye-glass when he designedly approached any one. As for Nettine, she did not bow and she did not smile, and she had no eye-glass nor trinket whatsoever to play with; but she fixed her eyes on his face, and bent a little forward, as to hear what he had to say, in a manner that really did not want prettiness.

"Mademoiselle Nettine," said the old gentleman, "has now on two occasions afforded me so much pleasure that if I knew of anything that could give mademoiselle pleasure, I should ask permission of Mrs. Arnold to present it."

Thus saying, and still smiling, still playing with his eye-glass, he began to occupy the chair by her side. The young girl's perfect repose, when she was in repose, was a *trait*, and though her lips were a little open, and her eyelids fully so, her beautiful hands lay as still as marble in her lap. On one wrist she wore a little ornament of Caroline's hair, but on the other she wore nothing, and it was to this last that, as Mr. Templar lowered his person, his regards likewise descended.

"A bracelet, for instance," he said, "though it could not add anything to so charming an arm, would at least remind mademoiselle of my gratitude."

The young lady's looks took the direction of his own, but without, it seemed, any extraordinary pleasure brightening them. A hair bracelet, she thought to herself, was not a very pretty thing. She liked this one because the hair was Caroline's, but—and then she lifted her eyes to the old gentleman's peruke.

What had not that lifting of the eyes to answer for? Their meaning, had Mr. Templar understood it, could not have delighted him; but the eyes themselves did, and he waxed enthusiastic and extravagant.

" If," he said, " there were anything you liked better. What *would* you like?"

" I should like," replied Nettine, without a moment's hesitation, " I should like a head-thing like the one worn by the lady on the front bench near the piano at Miss Mackenzie Browne's."

The old gentleman's regards fell; so did his countenance. "That," he said gravely, after a pause of three or four seconds, " was a diamond circlet."

" Well—I should like a diamond circlet."

" And the lady who wore it," he said, still more gravely, " was the Lady Anne Wing."

" Yes—Lady Anne Wing. I looked at nothing else all the evening."

" But you could not look at one on your own head. A diamond ring, now—"

" Oh, I should not care for a diamond ring ! I should like a diamond circlet !" persisted Nettine ; and then, seeing the gravity of the old gentleman's countenance, and reminding herself (for she was not after all, you see, as stupid as she was ignorant) of the gravity of his tone, she added,

" But perhaps only ladies like Lady Anne Wing wear diamond circlets ?"

" Rich people of all grades wear them," replied Mr. Templar ; and this was intelligible.

Nettine could well understand a trinket being too expensive. She, therefore, only looked away disappointed, and said no more ; while the old *fanatico*, now that her lustrous eyes were turned in another direction, glanced from time to time furtively at her side face, and from thence downwards to her quiet hands. And at every glance his little yellow-ish grey eye became less keen and more thoughtful, till at length, in rising when the duet was about to come to an end, he said, something in the manner of one speaking of a coral necklace to a child—

" We will think about this circlet !"—— and moved away, and took up a position nearer to the pianoforte. Nor did he again approach her otherwise than to make his parting compliments : and, notwithstanding the rather wistful look that accompanied Nettine's " good-night," I do not think she gathered any extraordinary encouragement from his peculiar smile, and the manner in which his little yellowish eyes fixed them-selves on her face ; nor even from the fact that those little yellowish eyes and that familiar smile continued to be fixed on her during his subsequent colloquy with the Professor, and that she was the last object on which they rested as he quitted the room.

CHAPTER VIII.

A FIANCÉE.

ABOUT a quarter-past two o'clock of the day
but one succeeding that on which Mr.
Templar's visit had been made, Miss Datchet
might have been seen to emerge from the Professor's gate. The afternoon was cold and
sunless, and rain or even snow seemed probable, yet no little wonted air of indecision
appeared. If the eyes of the young lady
took, in the first instance, the direction of
Camden Crescent, it was but for a moment,

and involuntarily. She closed the gate at once, and turned to the left in the manner of one who had not just then either leisure or mind for affectations.

She had not taken half a dozen steps when the well-known voice of the gate four doors off made itself heard, and Anastasia Collins, smartly dressed for a promenade, appeared at it. Caroline had no thought but of pausing to shake hands, and had even withdrawn one hand from her muff when the sauciest nod imaginable from Anastasia, who made not a step forward, defeated her intention, and caused her to pass on with a movement something similar to that of her former friend, and a face crimson with mortification, anger, and, subsequently, regret. It was the first time that Anastasia had evinced any distinct resentment of the disapproval of her own conduct indicated by Mr. and Mrs. Arnold in their prohibition of Caroline's visits, and it had taken the latter by surprise. Nevertheless, a very little reflection showed her that she had no right to wonder at it. She reminded herself with no little pain that much attention, almost kindness, to herself had at no time been sufficiently reciprocated, and might easily, in the matter of Sir Walter Wing, be held by the Collins's themselves to have met an ungrateful return. They could not, it is true, attribute this to Caroline: her own pleasure, nay, her own interests, had suffered too severely. But it was human nature, her heart reminded her, and the Collins's nature, her observation convinced her, to resent it to the person who would suffer from the resentment most. In sorrow, therefore, rather than in anger, and with the sort of half-awakened sense of fear that an amiable and non-combative person begins to entertain in conjunction with the discovery that she has acquired an enemy, Caroline walked forward to the place of meeting; at which corner when she arrived she encountered the sharp wind from which the houses had in a measure sheltered her, a tolerable foretaste of

March dust, and no dragoon officer whatever.

He had never yet failed her, and therefore, though the appointment had been a less distinct one than usual, she continued for some time to hope for his appearance on the scene, and likewise to combat loyally and with high courage an insidious presentiment of evil striving for admittance into her mind. It was not till the hour named by Rolleston as that after which he was not to be expected, was long past, that she quitted her post and entered the familiar green lane to let fall those first few tears in which so many precious things of youth are carried out of the heart for ever.

And now the reader very naturally and very properly supposes he is about to hear that Caroline went home. I regret to say she did not. I regret to say she inopportunely reminded herself of some ribbon or pair of gloves essential to her toilette on that particular afternoon ; and, notwithstanding the

uninviting aspect of the weather, she passed
the turning by which she might have reached
her own gate, and continued to pursue the
way that would lead her to the town. At the
foot of the steep hill upon which the gardens
at the back of Camden Place opened she
again encountered a cloud of dust.

" I think we may have snow, Tomkins !"
she said, to a chairman who stood at the
corner.

" Rain, Miss," replied the man.

A young lady, however, will expose herself
to the chance of rain when shopping is in
question, and Caroline proceeded.

At every crossing she had something to
resist, but at the corner of Prince's Buildings
she could not close her eyes soon enough to
prevent them from being almost blinded by
the dust, while a sort of twirl of the wind
nearly carried her silk skirt over her head.
The little occurrence seemed the more vexa-
tious when, having restored her dress to its
propriety, and recovered something of her

powers of vision, she beheld Rolleston — who must twenty seconds before have been approaching her from the locality of the Park — in the act of turning his horse into Milsom Street. He was riding slowly and with (she knew him so well and was not in the least near sighted) a somewhat occupied and thoughtful air which became likewise her own. She had been almost in the act of crossing over towards Milsom Street herself; but now her intentions suffered a change. There was a momentary indecision, and then she proceeded down Broad Street. Remember, I do not approve; I only recount.

And to those who know Bath, I need scarcely say that at the corners of Green Street and New Bond Street Miss Datchet's eyes, charming, notwithstanding the dust, took in one sense a right direction. Nay, at the corner of the last mentioned her steps took the same. The horseman, however, always sought by those charming eyes, was not found by them, and the young lady, contradicted in a reasonable expectation, was more severely annoyed—so she told herself—than she ought to have been.   Yet we may well pity her,— that is, if we have begun to comprehend that the dragoon officer was more to her than even ambition.   Nor, in attempting to comprehend it must we employ our own estimate of Captain Rolleston. Love, I suspect, is equally love, whether it be the creation of a pair of auburn whiskers and a spotless boot, or of all the fine qualities our notions of an admirable Crichton include.

This little Caroline had been seeing Rolleston, on an average, twice, for two hours at a time, in every week for the last three months; and now during the next fortnight she was not to see him at all. We may well suppose, then, that half a dozen words from him on this day preceding the one of his departure, nay, even such a look as she might hope to receive, would have contributed to her comfort in the interval. It was not so to be, however. She had wretchedly mistaken the purpose of his ride, and miscalculated its direction. Wretchedly but naturally she had believed him on his way to Pulteney Street, to Johnston Street, to Sydney Place. It had seemed to her so very probable he would be leaving cards in those localities. She did not soon entirely give up the reasonable expectation. She lingered, hoping against hope that he might still come round the corner which she only doubled—and that a little hurriedly— herself when impelled by the sudden recollection that, if detained in Milsom Street, he might have taken the nearest turning to the *Castle* during what would have to be, in that case, considered her very unfortuitous pause in the parallel thoroughfare.

Milsom Street was almost empty. Here and there a carriage, its drab-coated footman on the pavement beside it, was drawn up in front of a shop door; a few muffled pedestrians moved to and fro; a cab rattled over the stones; but not a single horseman was in sight.

It was not in Milsom Street that she would most have wished to encounter the object of her thoughts and hopes, yet she would have been thankful, only too thankful, in her extremity, to have met him even there; and the sight of that thinly-peopled promenade, in which he was not to be discovered, inflicted a severe pang on her heart. Conscientiously to discharge the duty that she had suffered herself to believe directed her steps in the first instance towards the town, she crossed over to Jolly's, and, with tears in her voice, asked for the ribbon she required. Nay, in occupying the chair placed for her, I think it was not quite without difficulty that she refrained from a little second act of the performance that had commenced an hour earlier in the familiar green lane.

Nevertheless, she bought her ribbon, and it was during a delay caused by the shopman in seeking gloves of the particular shade for which she had asked, that the increased number of foot-passengers in the street made her aware that the afternoon's concert at the Pump-room had come to an end. Simultaneously a conviction in regard to a certain individual entered her understanding ; a conviction moreover, she had scarcely commenced to entertain, when a party of persons the most interesting in the world to her appeared in sight. They were Sir Walter Wing, a lady, and her two beautiful daughters, well known in the little gay world of Bath, and— Rolleston : and of these, the Baronet, whose peculiar features, rather unpleasant countenance, and *distingué* air rendered him easily recognizable, offered his wonted civilities— rather earnestly it seemed to Caroline—at the side of Miss Agatha Meredith, while the dragoon officer was in attendance on Mrs. Meredith and her somewhat less handsome elder daughter.

In beholding a spectacle for which she had so little prepared herself, the heart of our poor Caroline suffered its first acutely jealous pang. Mrs. and the Misses Meredith were the wife and daughters of a gentleman who possessed one of the best houses in Brock Street, a fine income, and the most elegant equipage in Bath. You will perceive, then, that it must have been difficult for Caroline, without the guilt of covetousness, to contemplate a social position that commanded, so to speak, the attentions she was so grateful to receive. Alas! in a second gaze she would have been glad to assure herself that it did command, and only command, these attentions. The very few moments had shown her Rolleston at his best, while to the smiles of both mother and daughter she was unable to deny a charm that might as easily engage as command.

The time had arrived when she must leave the shop, and as it was probable that Captain Rolleston might not accompany his friends beyond the top of the street, she had a fair chance of meeting him on his return. This, however, in the discomposure of which she was very conscious, she could scarcely desire to do; in a manner, withal, so unexpected by him and so exposed to the observation of others. For an instant she thought she would proceed home by the way she came; but curiosity, anxiety to know whether he would make his bow at the top of the street, or accompany the Merediths further, prevailed; and, at a considerable distance, she followed the little group of persons, of whom only Rolleston himself, walking at the outer edge of the pavement and flourishing a little the gold-mounted riding-whip he so often carried, was visible to her eyes.

At the corner, she lost him, nor could she discover that any such pause took place as his parting compliments might have occasioned. Nevertheless, you will imagine the eagerness with which, despite her previous hesitation, her eyes sought his returning form. It did not appear; and when she herself arrived at the same corner she beheld without difficulty the whole party continuing its way along George Street.

Hope was no longer possible, and it would have been clearly indelicate to follow him further. In pursuing, however, the opposite direction, she more than once, more than twice paused for an instant to look round. He would perhaps make his adieu at the *next* corner, and a little beyond the entrance to the York House she lingered to watch proceedings. That final look showed him to her in the act of crossing over, still at the side of Miss Rose Meredith, to Gay Street. There was no longer any thing to retard her steps, and, believing she had surprised a smile of something like intelligence on the face of a chairman at the corner, she went on her way, but not exactly rejoicing.

The poor young lady, had, you perceive, suffered more than a disappointment; she had, in some sort, experienced a revelation. In Mrs. Collins's drawing-room, and in the Charlecombe lanes, the social distance between Rolleston and herself had been at its least. Nay, it had been at a distance known rather

than felt, nominal rather than real.   Till this
afternoon, she had never beheld him in the
society of young women in his own rank in
life.   I am justified therefore in speaking of
a revelation.   It was the unaccustomed spectacle of a lover so near and yet so remote that
had shown the disadvantages of her position,
—the unfriended, unsupported character of
her claim.   I say not whether she magnified
these disadvantages.   In ascending Belvedere
she told herself that she *did*, and taxed herself with unreasonableness, jealousy, and ill-
temper.   Yet the sort of depression she was
resisting is not as often unreasonable as it is accused of being so.   Frequently, it is produced
by the exercise of a latent judgment juster
than that we ordinarily employ.   Caroline,
however, possessed not an analytical turn of
mind, and *did* possess a bright and loyal
heart, and, disappointed, mortified, pained as
she had been, was able to convince herself
in entering the Professor's gate, that the disappointment, the mortification and the pain,

new to her and sufficiently unpleasant to suffer, were, after all, but temporary affairs that
a little reflection would alleviate, and a fortnight, at the worst and at the latest, entirely
dispel.

Indisposed, nevertheless, to encounter without a little further preparation of countenance
the scrutiny of the maternal eye, Miss Datchet
evoked no sounds that were unnecessary from
either gate or house-door, and ascended immediately the stairs.   On the upper flight of
these she met the servant Marianne, who had
just (probably at the footstep of Caroline herself) emerged from the apartment of Mademoiselle.   She had left the door of this
apartment a little open behind her, and an
unusually bright light from within impelling
Caroline to enter, the extraordinary spectacle
of an attic illuminated by several pieces of
candle, and of Nettine standing in her white
petticoat before the little looking glass, and
in the act of holding, with arms bare and of
a dazzling whiteness, a tiara of brilliants

above her forehead, presented itself to her view.

" But — good gracious!" exclaimed Caroline, otherwise speechless with an astonishment that was not decreased by the immediate rejoinder of Nettine.

"Is it not?" said the latter, turning on her visitor a face whose beauty was only now fully comprehended by Caroline, "is is not beautiful? Do you see how bright it makes one's eyes? Those bracelets, too," and here the regards of Miss Datchet fell on more diamonds, flashing from an open case on the dressing table, "they are all mine—given me by Mr. Templar."

" Mr. Templar!"

" He has asked me in marriage—this old man who is so rich. Oh! do you see that violet colour? and now it is green! I am to be his wife."

CHAPTER IX.

MISS MONTRESOR.

"But, mamma," said Caroline, a day or two after this, when all seemed quite settled, when Mr. Templar and Mr. Arnold had held another and a longer interview, when the former had passed an evening in Mrs. Arnold's drawing-room in the character of the *fiancé* of Mademoiselle Nettine, when Mademoiselle had slept—so Marianne protested and the family believed—in her diamond circlet, and Miss Datchet herself had found time, at little intervals, to recover from her first astonishment, and arrange her ideas—

" But, mamma—"

" Well, child ?"

" This marriage seems to me a strange one. I could not have married Mr. Templar."

" Then," Mrs. Arnold replied, a little drily, " it is very lucky you are not asked to do so."

In a general way Miss Datchet would have been amused by her mother's speech. On this particular occasion, however, the rather anxious gravity of her countenance did not relax even into a smile.

" But, do you not wonder that Nettine is so very ready to do so ?"

" No," replied Mrs. Arnold, biting off the thread of her seam, " I do not wonder at it at all. And it is not neccessary that you should go putting such a notion into her head. I don't see what you have to do with it."

" No, but—"

" Bless the girl, with her ' buts !' Every one is not to think that Captain Rolleston is all the world."

" Of course not."

" Well, then ?"

A little silence ensued, presently broken again by Caroline.

" Do you know," she said, " that to-morrow will be her birthday—her seventeenth birth-day ?"

" I heard you say so."

"I wish, mamma, she was not quite so young.   Don't you ?"

" No," replied Mrs. Arnold, and bit off another thread. " Your father thinks her youth a point in her favour; in favour of her happiness, I mean."

" If she could be sure that she knows what she is about."

" What should hinder her to know what she is about?" demanded Mrs. Arnold, almost angrily.   " I think she knows very well what she is about—a great deal better than you do. I only hope it mayn't turn out so."

" Never mind about me, mamma, just now. I dare say I may not be very wise. But— when Nettine first came here, you remember you thought her very odd and unlike other people. Now, I have come to think the same. I think her very odd and very unlike other people; and in this matter, especially, I think her very odd and very unlike indeed."

"Then I am sure," Mrs. Arnold replied, "we have the greater reason to be thankful. The more odd she is, the more her need of a good home and somebody to take care of her."

"That is true."

"We cannot keep her always; and the more odd she is, the less she is fit to go out into the world to get her own living."

"That is very true," Caroline again said, after a thoughtful little silence. "Do you think it is this that weighs with papa?"

"I have no doubt of it. Not that I can see what you mean, or that any 'weight' is wanted. Everybody must think that it is a wonderful piece of good fortune for a girl like Nettine. And you will find that everybody

will think so, and call us all the intriguers
and schemers in the world for having brought
it about. But that won't break our backs.
And I wonder you don't see, Caroline, how
it may be a good card dealt to your hand."

"I do see that."

"Pray has Rolleston gone away without
saying anything of what he thinks to do."

"He is only gone away for a fortnight."

"With Mr. Templar marrying Nettine, and
Sir Walter Wing Anastasia, the deuce is in it
if you ain't good enough for Rolleston. And
I should let him know it too, in your place."

"Heigho!" said Caroline, and the subject
having taken this unexpected turn, she moved
away, while her mother stirred the fire.

Caroline did see the advantages to herself
that might reasonably be expected from this
marriage of Nettine to Mr. Templar. Yet
the prsopect neither warped her judgment
nor reconciled her mind. "I could not have
married him," her heart was constantly re-
peating; and it seemed to her the most ex-

traordinary thing in the world that Nettine could.

And so readily. The young lady of twenty found herself able to comprehend—not in her own case, because of Rolleston, but in the case of another—the possibility of succumbing to persuasion, to argument, to fear of the future, to temptations—skilfully offered—of ease, position, and wealth. But nothing of this had been needed. Nettine's marriage would, indeed, give her the good things I have mentioned; but then they were not things to Nettine. They were not understood by her. They were words that had no meaning for her. She was marrying—Caroline told herself, and with an astonishment that even exceeded her sense of wrong—for a diamond circlet ;—simply for a diamond circlet, and nothing else.

And then the daughter of Mrs. Arnold was as sensible as her mother that worldliness and successful scheming would be attributed to them. This seemed the more certain when it was found that Mr. Templar would require the engagement to remain a profound secret up to the moment of the marriage. The probable dissatisfaction, he stated to Mr. Arnold, of relations of his, who would regard the connection as prejudicial to their own interests, rendered it undesirable for him to make known his intentions; and to a man of his age, and one so unquestionably his own master, the Arnolds had no reasonable objection to offer. Nay, I think that, on reflection, this required secresy was not distasteful to themselves. It would prevent all remonstrance, while remonstrance might be supposed likely to avail, all pre-judgment of the affair by society at large, and all such questions on the part of their own immediate friends as they might not have been disposed or able to reply to. Caroline Datchet was the person whom the clandestine engagement could most embarrass, and this for a reason that will presently be obvious to the reader. The marriage of Nettine to Mr. Templar was fixed

for a day exactly three weeks subsequent to
the date of that gentleman's proposals; the
return of Captain Rolleston might be expected
to precede, by about six days, the marriage.
In the walks, therefore, to be hoped for in
the course of those intervening days, Caroline's enforced want of candour must be certainly painful, and possibly, injurious to herself.

The young lady's good star, however, took
the matter under its own control, and at the
expiration of the fortnight, Rolleston did not
return.   Never was uneasiness at the pro-
longed absence of a lover so largely counteracted by an opposite feeling.   The important day now drew so near that Caroline
began to find herself able to hope that it
might arrive before Rolleston ; and this
every hour seemed to render more probable.
Fortunately, she had just now less time than
usual to bestow on the affairs of her heart.
You will easily comprehend that her brides-
maid's dress would occupy her to some extent,

and the claims of the bridal *trousseau* on her taste, judgment, and admiration, to an extent still greater.

For a *trousseau*, and one unpresented by her *futur*, Nettine was to have. She had been but a few months an inmate of her uncle's house, and three fourths of the sum he had received with her remained in his hands. In the time, then, between the two interviews held by him with Mr. Templar, he (Mr. Arnold) had written to his sister, and received the following reply.

"MY DEAR ARNOLD—

"Your letter is in my hand. I can in nowise receive back the money, or any part of it. It was paid to you to provide the child Antoinette with the means of earning her bread. If you have provided for her in marriage, it is equal. Requite yourself to the uttermost farthing, and deal with the remainder as you think right.

"Further, I have a request to make. Let

me hear no more. It seems I may linger, yet I shall not have too much time to set in order my house, meaning my soul. Connected with this subject is much that disturbs and withdraws and tortures me. Present it not again to my mind. My illness may be longer or shorter, but its termination is sure. Let this, Arnold, be our last communication on earth. If I ever enter Heaven we shall meet, and there will be ' no more sea.'

" Yours,

" FANNY."

" London."

The final renunciation of Nettine contained in this letter, the substance of which (not the letter itself) was put before Mr. Templar by Mr. Arnold, could hardly be displeasing to the former gentleman.

" An eccentric person!" he said. " Most estimable, evidently, but eccentric; and probably under sectarian influence, with which—"

A bland wave of the hand dismissed the matter at this point, as one which none but the estimable person herself could by possibility understand, or have any concern in. With regard to the money, Mr. Arnold would gratify him by not recurring to it. His (the professor's) good wife was in possession of his wishes respecting the young lady's *trousseau*. He begged to repeat, he offered her *carte blanche*. Mr. Arnold was indisposed to accept the responsibility of applying this trifling sum? Let him then (Mr. Templar) suggest a wedding present from Mademoiselle to her cousin.

Mr. Arnold was, however, still indisposed.

"Under the circumstances," he said, "it would be impossible for him or any part of his family to appropriate the money."

Twice he said "under the circumstances," and Mr. Templar again waved his hand, and with an air that was not altogether well-pleased.

—In that case—Mr. Arnold could, of course,

best judge of possibilities;—in that case Mrs. Arnold would perhaps be so good as to expend the money on the travelling requirements of the young lady; and the wardrobe *he* should order would wait their arrival in Paris.

This was in all respects a satisfactory arrangement, and on the wedding day a costly bracelet, presented by the bridegroom—with whom a bracelet seemed an uppermost idea —to Caroline, was intended to compensate to her for the fastidious scruples of her stepfather. But this is anticipating.

One evening in the commencement of the week that was to make Mr. Templar "the happiest of men" he, drinking his cup of tea in Mrs. Arnold's now habitually occupied drawing-room, said—

"Ladies, I am going to a wedding tomorrow."

"A wedding!" Miss Datchet exclaimed. "Dear me! Whose?"

"I confide it to your discretion—Miss Montresor's."

"You don't say so! I had no idea it was to be so soon. Yet, now you speak of it, I met Miss Montresor yesterday walking with a gentleman who must have been Lord Arden."

"Lord Douglas Arden!"

"Lord Douglas Arden. Such an elegant man! What a handsome couple they will make. And of course it is to be a very grand wedding?"

"It is to be a very gay one. You should be amongst the spectators."

"Oh! we will," Caroline readily replied, for his glance had included the lady of his love. "I am so glad you mentioned it; otherwise we should not have known. Nettine has never seen a wedding."

Here the old gentleman returned his tea-cup to the table, and in so doing whispered a few words to his *fiancée,* at which I have an idea the latter was expected to blush, but did not.

" And at what time," Miss Datchet asked, " is it to be ?"

" Ten is the hour named; but you should be there earlier to get a good place."

" Much earlier, I should think. Quite an hour earlier. Nettine, we must be there by nine o'clock. At Walcot Church ?"

" At Walcot Church."

They were not "there," however, by nine o'clock, and if they had been, would not, I think, have got a very good place. At any rate, by the time they did arrive the church was crowded to a degree quite natural and reasonable on the occasion of the marriage of Miss Montresor to a lord; and, no seat whatever being obtainable, Caroline was grateful to be compensated for about forty minutes of considerable suffering in the back of the gallery by a doubtful and momentary glimpse of the white satin of the bride as it swept up the aisle. As for Nettine, unac-

customed and bewildered, she saw nothing.
They might hear—that is to say, they might
have heard if the persons around them had
been more impressed by the fact that they
were within the walls of a church, and had
talked and laughed less loudly. Besides
hearing—for in those days choral weddings
were not—hearing offered no extreme temptation to remain, and Caroline, who was a
frequenter of weddings, whispered Nettine
that by a timely withdrawal they might secure,
near the gate through which the marriage
cortége must pass to its carriages, an eventual
sight of all that was to be seen.

Nettine had no objection to offer, and they
began to effect a retrograde movement
through the crowd ; but did not, nevertheless,
gain the desired point very many minutes too
soon. They found the concourse of persons
outside the church doors very great,—so great,
indeed, that, notwithstanding they joined it
from within, they had no little difficulty in
maintaining a position in the foremost ranks.

They were pushed, they were elbowed, they were trodden on, but the struggle, though severe, was not of long duration; and I can only hope they felt themselves amply rewarded when the satin folds of the bridal robe touched, in passing them, their skirts of a less costly fabric. The enthusiasm of the crowd was great; delight was in every eye, praise on every lip. Sometimes, even on such occasions, amid the general approval the ear is made aware of individual discontent. But not on this. It was acclamation, and no wonder!

"An't she the moral of one, ma'am?" exclaimed an excited bystander to Caroline. "An't she the pictur' of a bride?" And Caroline could delightedly reply, "She is, indeed!"

And she was, indeed; or if not the picture of a bride, she was the bride of a picture. We have all seen her! In oils, in water-colours, in engravings, on the walls of the exhibition of the Royal Academy, on our own drawing-room tables in the keepsakes and books of beauty and literary souvenirs of that day. She was tall and elegant, and fair as a pearl, with oval face, and a faint blush on her cheek, and eyes fixed on the ground, and a sweet, serious expression; and her white glove rested lightly on the sleeve of the bridegroom, who owed it, I think, chiefly to this that his good looks were observed at all, for who regards a bridegroom? Yet the bridegroom of Miss Montresor was a fine, tall young man, a full head taller than herself, with nobly cut features, and dark, glossy whiskers and hair, with the bearing of a soldier and a gentleman, and a toilette the faultless result of an admirable taste, even though it was his wedding day. As a mere bridegroom, indeed, he might not have received much attention; but the same delighted bystander who had been enthusiastic in praise of the lady, now confidently imparted to Caroline his entire approval of her choice, and pronounced him "the very pictur of a lord."

Nettine, less at home than her companion in the crowd, could make but little of the spectacle. She did not even know that the person on whose arm the bride emerged from the church door must necessarily be the bridegroom; and when, being impelled almost into the path of the wedding party by the pressure from behind, her shoulder was touched by the elbow of a tall, light-haired, aristocratic looking personage who, on the point of entering one of the carriages, turned quite round, and with an unmistakable sincerity of solicitude, to apologise for the accident, she believed herself face to face with Lord Douglas Arden. Caroline corrected her mistake.

"That," said Miss Datchet, "was Colonel Montresor, the father of the bride? You did not grant him pardon. It was a little clumsy of him, it is true. Did he hurt you at all?"

And Nettine replied that he did not.

CHAPTER X.

A LETTER.

From Colonel Montresor to the Hon. Augustus Damer.

" A thousand thanks, my dear Damer, for Lady Emily's congratulations, and for yours. You both comprehend me perfectly. Desolate as Susan's marriage leaves me (without a real interest or object in the world,) I should abhor myself if I could regret it. She has chosen where I can with all my soul approve; and you who have witnessed portions of my anxiety for the motherless girl, comprehend with the less difficulty how great a burden the painful ceremony of Tuesday has lifted from my mind. Nevertheless, with the burden, 'Othello's occupation's gone.'

"As to the affair that separated us so suddenly, it is not now worth speaking of. Your informant, however, was correct,—an impression had been made on the child's fancy; and, for the gentleman—it was as I suspected.

"On my arrival in the Rue ——, I found Susan had gone with Madame de Séran to a ball at the Hotel de M., and to the Hotel de M. I followed her. Madame la Baronne was almost the first person of my acquaintance I beheld; and she was evidently confounded. 'She dances,' she replied to my inquiry, 'with a countryman of her own—a charming young English officer, and the partner for the adorable Susan, the most unexceptionable in the world.' I bowed, and passed on to seek my daughter.

" A first glance sufficiently convinced me that the person bending over her was the same Mr. Paul Vaughan of whom I spoke to you at Interlachen.   I had not seen him since he was brought to a juvenile ball at my house in London, but I recognized him immediately. Susan was listening to him with pink cheeks and downcast eyes; and, struck with the difference between this and her ordinary aspect, I said to myself as I looked with serious anxiety upon the pair: ' God forbid she should love this man !'

" I drew her arm within my own, and for a few minutes we all conversed together. The countenance of Mr. Vaughan evinced very little pleasure at my arrival.   I found in what he said a certain underbred hauteur and a captious disposition to take offence.   I alluded in no way on that night to what I had heard or seen, but the next morning I spoke frankly to Susan on the subject. She was embarrassed; her voice faltered; at length, with more energy than I expected from her, she threw herself on my breast and avowed a preference for Mr. Paul Vaughan. I had by this time learned all that was necessary to assure me of the personal unworthiness of the man who, as the near relation of my Lord Featherstone, must have been repugnant to me; and on such ground could have no doubt of the result. I spoke to her very tenderly; therefore I took blame to myself for having quitted Paris even for so short a time, and by my absence exposed her to the attentions of persons who could not, had I been present, have approached her. I pointed out to her that there was nothing in the position, little in the prospects, of Mr. Vaughan to entitle him to aspire to her hand. I told her that since her happiness was my first object, this inferiority was not my greatest objection to the gentleman in question.

"' Ah, papa! what other?' was her naïve inquiry.

"' Antecedents of his,' I replied, ' offer me no security that your happiness will be well placed in his keeping.'

" ' Ah ! I think he feared those antecedents. But he has promised so solemnly.'

" What he had promised I did not think it necessary to hear. I imparted to her what had reached me of his temper, and, if I mistake not, she was already aware that injustice had not been done him in that respect. I touched on a certain rather unusual inelegance of language and address, and her blushes admitted the truth of the criticism. I alluded to her own large fortune as offering a temptation to an expensive man, and she protested indignant disbelief. I spoke of a propensity for the turf and billiard table, and she let fall a few tears.

" I spare you further details of a very long conversation. From the first, I entertained no doubt of being able in a little while to eradicate an impression which Madame de Séran had, it was tolerably clear to me, been doing her possible to render a serious one. The young gentleman himself afforded me valuable help.

" Three days after my return to Paris,

while Susan and I sat chatting at a breakfast, in her dressing-room, succeeding a late ball, I remarked that Mademoiselle Hortense, her French waiting-maid, took the liberty of entering two or three times the room on as many rather frivolous errands, and that she seemed anxious to attract her mistress's notice without exposing herself to mine. I took up my newspaper, and so altered the position of my chair as to turn my shoulder on Miss Hortense and her young lady, while I at the same time fixed my eyes on a large looking-glass which reflected all that was passing in the room. I had no sooner done this than Mademoiselle coughed, twirled herself round, shook a little bunch of keys she carried in her hand, and, in the end, succeeded in diverting my daughter's attention from the kitten in her lap. Then I saw the corner of a letter peeping from one of the pockets of her smart apron.

"Susan opened her eyes in astonishment at the grimaces of the *soubrette*, and, notwithstanding the pantomine of the latter behind my chair, asked simply and aloud—

" ' What is the matter with you, Hortense?'

" ' Mademoiselle Hortense,' I said, without turning, ' has a letter for you, my love!'

" The girl coloured violently, and in a tone of denial exclaimed—

" ' A letter!'

" ' In the pocket of your apron. Be so good as to put it on the table.'

" She did so in sheer confusion, and, scarlet to the ears, tripped out of the room.

" Then I resumed my old position.

" ' Susan,' I said, ' the letter that lies there is addressed to you by Mr. Vaughan, who has bribed Hortense to put it into your hands unseen by me.'

" ' Impossible!' she exclaimed.

" ' Seeking,' I continued, ' to make you a party with a little French chamber-maid and himself, to a transaction which would have the effect of placing you in her power and his own.'

"'Impossible!' Susan again exclaimed, but with, notwithstanding, an uneasy glance towards the document in question. 'Oh, papa! it is impossible!'

" 'Open it, love, and see.'

" With trembling fingers she broke the seal.

"'Well, Susan!'

" The colour mounted rapidly into her face as she glanced over it.

"'Take it, papa! Burn it! and, if you please, we will not mention his name again.'

"'In that case,' I said, 'we will do better than burn it. I feel certain that a letter conveyed to you in this manner can contain no sentiments that will not inspire you with aversion and contempt.'

" That same evening the young gentleman had his love missive returned to him in an envelope, within which was written the following lines—

" 'Colonel Montresor returns the enclosed letter by the desire of his daughter.'

" And thus ended an affair that had occasioned me an anxiety as painful as short lived.

"We went, as you know, to Florence; and I selected Douglas Arden from the little court that presently assembled round the child. I saw with pleasure that she herself began to distinguish him from other aspirants. I did not err in telling myself that her taste would enable her to appreciate the difference between her new lover and her former one, and soon found that any allusion which could remind her of her repented preference covered her cheeks with blushes of annoyance and vexation. In due time the lover asked my august permission to place himself at Miss Susan's feet, and the permission was cheerfully accorded. From that day to the one of their wedding the young *fiancés* and their affairs have occupied my thoughts and time, and it is only now that I begin to have leisure to look about me.

"I return to the continent. Well!—you are disappointed. But it must be so. The lawyers cannot, however, at this moment, do without me; and it is expected and right that I should meet the newly married pair at

Studleigh before I depart. Now, what are your summer plans? What have you against accompanying me? The gout? It is an argument in my favour!—and a fellow who has been for more than half a score of years head nurse to a delicate fine lady is qualified to be careful of a gouty gentleman. But, if you plead Lady Emily, who will not herself be tempted across the Channel, I must be content. You have indeed a fair excuse for remaining by your own hearth. Long may you be able to offer it !

" Rawlins has this moment brought me the extraordinary intelligence that at nine o'clock this morning, and in Walcot Church, our old friend Templar married a young French girl of sixteen, the relative, or pupil, or both, of a professor of music in this place. The man I know, and respect highly enough to increase the surprise with which I have received the information. With the ladies of his family I have no acquaintance. The secrecy observed in the affair looks badly. It must be remembered, however, that Templar is neither in his first nor second childhood.   There seems no reason to doubt Rawlins' authority.   By and bye, I shall hear further particulars at the club.

*   *   *   *

" Since writing the above I have, I believe, heard all there is to hear. It is not much. The marriage has taken place as stated. The bride—whether French or English seems doubtful—is the niece and pupil of the person I mentioned, and made a *début* as a public singer a few weeks since, in the drawing-rooms of a friend of mine, at a concert from which I was absent. She is seventeen, beautiful, and of character ; and will therefore, it is presumed, return from Paris—whither the happy pair have betaken themselves—to occupy a position amongst us. He has, I fear, relatives to whom the affair will be wholly unacceptable. All kind things to Lady Emily."

END OF VOL. I.

T. C. Newby, 30, Welbeck Street, Cavendish Square, London.

www.ingramcontent.com/pod-product-compliance
Lightning Source LLC
Chambersburg PA
CBHW031028120726
47905CB00007B/2085